P9-CCO-608

Teddy Fay hedges his bets in the latest thriller from #1 *New York Times* bestselling author Stuart Woods.

When Peter Barrington and Ben Bacchetti come under threat while working at a film festival abroad, Teddy Fay is lured to the glittering city of Macau to resolve the problem. He'll soon find that the world of posh casinos, luxurious developments, and boundless wealth has a dark underbelly of crime and political intrigue . . . and that the biggest players behind the scenes may be far closer to home than anticipated. With international deals and private vendettas at stake, the villains who engineered the plot aren't about to let Teddy stand in their way. What they don't know is that this seemingly harmless film producer has more than a few tricks up his sleeve.

Praise for the Stone Barrington Novels

Double Jeopardy

"A clever and captivating reading experience."
—Bookreporter.com

Hush-Hush

"Prime escapism from a master of the genre." —*Booklist*

Shakeup

"This is prime Woods. . . . Slick, reliable, action-oriented escapism, just right for troubled times." —*Booklist*

Choppy Water

"The action builds to a satisfying double climax"

—*Publishers Weekly*

Bombshell

"The perfect bonbon to pick up for distraction during those long production numbers at the actual Oscars."

—*Kirkus Reviews*

Hit List

"Fast-moving easy reading in the familiar Woods style."

—*Booklist*

Treason

"Bon appétit to readers who like their international intrigue sweet and weightless as a soufflé."

—*Kirkus Reviews*

Stealth

"Smooth, easy-reading escapism in the trademark Woods style."

—*Booklist*

Contraband

"Woods balances the criminal doings with loads of light banter and tantalizing glimpses of great sex."

—*Publishers Weekly*

Skin Game

"The ingenious ways in which Teddy outwits his adversaries is a large part of this entry's appeal. Series fans will hope he has a long career." —*Publishers Weekly*

Wild Card

"Woods shows no sign of flagging in this long-running series." —*Publishers Weekly*

A Delicate Touch

"Woods continues to deliver satisfying escapist fare, with the Bondian Barrington outmaneuvering his foes yet again, always with high tech gadgetry at the ready and a beautiful woman at his side." —*Booklist*

Desperate Measures

"Woods creates another action-packed thriller for his readers to devour, with plenty of interesting twists and turns that make for a nonstop, can't-catch-your-breath read."

—*Booklist*

Turbulence

"Inventive . . . [An] alluring world of wealth, power, and crime." —*Publishers Weekly*

Shoot First

"Smooth . . . The principal pleasure lies in watching the suave, resourceful Stone maintain his good humor and high lifestyle throughout all his travails."

—*Publishers Weekly*

Unbound

"Stuart Woods is a no-nonsense, slam-bang storyteller."

—*Chicago Tribune*

Quick & Dirty

"Suspenseful . . . The excitement builds."

—*Publishers Weekly*

Indecent Exposure

"[An] irresistible, luxury-soaked soap opera."

—*Publishers Weekly*

Fast & Loose

"Another entertaining episode in [a] soap opera about the rich and famous."

—Associated Press

Below the Belt

"Compulsively readable . . . [An] easy-reading page-turner."

—*Booklist*

Sex, Lies & Serious Money

"Series fans will continue to enjoy this bird's-eye view of the high life." —*Booklist*

Dishonorable Intentions

"Diverting." —*Publishers Weekly*

Family Jewels

"Mr. Woods knows how to portray the beautiful people, their manners and mores, their fluid and sparkling conversation, their easy expectations and all the glitter that surrounds and defines them. A master of dialogue, action and atmosphere, [Woods] has added one more jewel of a thriller-mystery to his ever-growing collection."

—*Fort Myers Florida Weekly*

Scandalous Behavior

"Addictive . . . Pick [*Scandalous Behavior*] up at your peril. You can get hooked." —*Lincoln Journal-Star*

Foreign Affairs

"Purrs like a well-tuned dream machine . . . Mr. Woods knows how to set up scenes and link them to keep the action, emotion, and information moving. He presents the places he takes us to vividly and convincingly. . . . Enjoy this slick thriller by a thoroughly satisfying professional."

—*Florida Weekly*

Hot Pursuit

"Fans will enjoy the vicarious luxury ride as usual."

—*Publishers Weekly*

Insatiable Appetites

"Multiple exciting story lines . . . Readers of the series will enjoy the return of the dangerous Dolce." —*Booklist*

Paris Match

"Plenty of fast-paced action and deluxe experiences that keep the pages turning. Woods is masterful with his use of dialogue and creates natural and vivid scenes for his readers to enjoy." —Myrtle Beach *Sun News*

Cut and Thrust

"This installment goes down as smoothly as a glass of Knob Creek." —*Publishers Weekly*

Carnal Curiosity

"Stone Barrington shows he's one of the smoothest operators around . . . Entertaining." —*Publishers Weekly*

Standup Guy

"Stuart Woods still owns an imagination that simply won't quit. . . . This is yet another edge-of-your-seat adventure."

—*Suspense Magazine*

Doing Hard Time

"Longtime Woods fans who have seen Teddy [Fay] evolve from a villain to something of a lovable antihero will enjoy watching the former enemies work together in this exciting yarn. Is this the beginning of a beautiful partnership? Let's hope so." —*Booklist*

Unintended Consequences

"Since 1981, readers have not been able to get their fill of Stuart Woods's *New York Times* best-selling novels of suspense." —*Orlando Sentinel*

Collateral Damage

"High-octane . . . Woods's blend of exciting action, sophisticated gadgetry, and last-minute heroics doesn't disappoint." —*Publishers Weekly*

Severe Clear

"Stuart Woods has proven time and time again that he's a master of suspense who keeps his readers frantically turning the pages." —Bookreporter.com

BOOKS BY STUART WOODS

FICTION

*Foul Play**
*Class Act**
*Double Jeopardy**
*Hush-Hush**
*Shakeup**
*Choppy Water**
*Hit List**
*Treason**
*Stealth**
*Contraband**
*Wild Card**
*A Delicate Touch**
*Desperate Measures**
*Turbulence**
*Shoot First**
*Unbound**
*Quick & Dirty**
*Indecent Exposure**
*Fast & Loose**
*Below the Belt**
*Sex, Lies & Serious Money**
*Dishonorable Intentions**
*Family Jewels**
*Scandalous Behavior**
*Foreign Affairs**
*Naked Greed**
*Hot Pursuit**
*Insatiable Appetites**
*Paris Match**
*Cut and Thrust**
*Carnal Curiosity**
*Standup Guy**
*Doing Hard Time**
*Unintended Consequences**
*Collateral Damage**
*Severe Clear**
*Unnatural Acts**
*D.C. Dead**
*Son of Stone**
*Bel-Air Dead**
*Strategic Moves**
Santa Fe Edge†
*Lucid Intervals**
*Kisser**
Hothouse Orchid‡
*Loitering with Intent**
Mounting Fears§
*Hot Mahogany**
Santa Fe Dead†
Beverly Hills Dead
*Shoot Him If He Runs**
*Fresh Disasters**
Short Straw†
*Dark Harbor**
Iron Orchid‡
*Two Dollar Bill**
The Prince of Beverly Hills
*Reckless Abandon**
Capital Crimes§
*Dirty Work**
Blood Orchid‡
*The Short Forever**
Orchid Blues‡
*Cold Paradise**
*L.A. Dead**
The Run§
*Worst Fears Realized**
Orchid Beach‡
*Swimming to Catalina**
*Dead in the Water**
*Dirt**
Choke

Imperfect Strangers
Heat
Dead Eyes
L.A. Times
Santa Fe Rules†
*New York Dead**
Palindrome
Grass Roots§
White Cargo
Deep Lie§
Under the Lake
Run Before the Wind§
Chiefs§

COAUTHORED BOOKS

*Jackpot*** (with Bryon Quertermous)
*Bombshell*** (with Parnell Hall)
*Skin Game*** (with Parnell Hall)
*The Money Shot*** (with Parnell Hall)
Barely Legal†† (with Parnell Hall)
*Smooth Operator*** (with Parnell Hall)

TRAVEL

A Romantic's Guide to the Country Inns of Britain and Ireland (1979)

MEMOIR

Blue Water, Green Skipper

**A Stone Barrington Novel*
†*An Ed Eagle Novel*
‡*A Holly Barker Novel*
§*A Will Lee Novel*
***A Teddy Fay Novel*
††*A Herbie Fisher Novel*

JACKPOT

STUART WOODS
AND BRYON QUERTERMOUS

G. P. PUTNAM'S SONS
NEW YORK

PUTNAM
— EST. 1838 —
G. P. PUTNAM'S SONS
Publishers Since 1838
An imprint of Penguin Random House LLC
penguinrandomhouse.com

Copyright © 2021 by Stuart Woods
Excerpt from *Class Act* copyright © 2021 by Stuart Woods
Penguin supports copyright. Copyright fuels creativity, encourages diverse voices, promotes free speech, and creates a vibrant culture. Thank you for buying an authorized edition of this book and for complying with copyright laws by not reproducing, scanning, or distributing any part of it in any form without permission. You are supporting writers and allowing Penguin to continue to publish books for every reader.

The Library of Congress has catalogued the
G. P. Putnam's Sons hardcover edition as follows:

Names: Woods, Stuart, author. | Quertermous, Bryon, author.
Title: Jackpot / Stuart Woods and Bryon Quertermous.
Description: New York: G. P. Putnam's Sons, 2021. | Series: A Teddy Fay novel.
Identifiers: LCCN 2021011959 (print) | LCCN 2021011960 (ebook) |
ISBN 9780593188453 (hardcover) | ISBN 9780593188477 (ebook)
Subjects: GSAFD: Suspense fiction. | Adventure fiction.
Classification: LCC PS3573.O642 J33 2021 (print) |
LCC PS3573.O642 (ebook) | DDC 813/.54—dc23
LC record available at https://lccn.loc.gov/2021011959
LC ebook record available at https://lccn.loc.gov/2021011960

First G. P. Putnam's Sons hardcover edition / June 2021
First G. P. Putnam's Sons premium edition / November 2021
G. P. Putnam's Sons premium edition ISBN: 9780593188460

Printed in the United States of America
1 3 5 7 9 10 8 6 4 2

BOOK DESIGN BY KRISTIN DEL ROSARIO

This is a work of fiction. Names, characters, places, and incidents either are the product of the author's imagination or are used fictitiously, and any resemblance to actual persons, living or dead, businesses, companies, events, or locales is entirely coincidental.

If you purchased this book without a cover, you should be aware that this book is stolen property. It was reported as "unsold and destroyed" to the publisher, and neither the author nor the publisher has received any payment for this "stripped book."

JACKPOT

1

TEDDY FAY JUST WANTED TO SLEEP. HE'D NEVER HAD TROUble sleeping, even in war zones and on the trail of high-profile targets. But a series of Hollywood scouting meetings across three continents in seven days in his identity as movie producer Billy Barnett had done him in.

He was in the first-class lounge at the Hong Kong airport waiting for the final leg of his flight back to Los Angeles, when he felt someone approaching. He ignored his instincts and closed his eyes tighter. When the sensation of being watched wouldn't go away, he opened his eyes just in time to see a face leaning in toward him.

In one motion, Teddy rolled off the leather couch he'd been curled up on and shot his right elbow out toward the face in front of him. When he hit the ground, he was fully awake and expected that to be the end of it. But the person was still there. It was an Asian woman with hard, beautiful features and a lithe frame. She took a step toward him and stretched out her hand. He swatted at her hand as he stood up, but instead of pulling away, she engaged with his hand and tugged his arm.

As Teddy fell toward the woman, he spun around so his back was facing her and dropped into a less than graceful version of the splits. He snapped his right leg back at the woman and swept her legs out from underneath her. Again, he expected that to be the end of it. If this woman was a thief looking for a quick score from a sleeping tourist, Teddy had made it very clear he was not an easy target. Since it was the middle of the night, there were only a few other people around, and all were absorbed in their own business. Maybe she would go away and pick a new victim.

Or maybe she wasn't trying to rob him. Maybe she was trying to kill him.

As far as Teddy knew, the short list of people looking to kill Billy Barnett had been taken care of back in Los Angeles. Was she there for Teddy? The list of people wanting to kill Teddy was more robust, but he wasn't traveling under that name and he'd taken great care to keep Teddy in the shadows as much as possible.

He never carried a gun when he was traveling on Centurion Studios business, and that had rarely been a problem. Now he was looking around the minimal furnishings of the lounge area to see if there was anything he could use as a weapon, but his thought process kept being interrupted by the woman repeatedly coming at him.

Teddy rolled around the floor away from her approaches, quickly processing his surroundings. Before he'd settled on a course of action, he saw security approaching and, for once, he was happy to see armed guards in uniform. He stopped rolling and lay flat on his back, waiting for the guards to take the woman away. But they came for him, too. He saw the Tasers just before he felt them, and then he was finally asleep.

◆ ◆ ◆

"I wasn't attacking him, I was trying to wake him," Teddy heard a woman say in clear English.

He opened his eyes and saw he was in a brightly lit small office that looked like a bathroom with all the fixtures removed. An enormous man in a pristine white security uniform with thick black hair and a thin, drooping moustache sat behind a desk with a gold nameplate that read SERGEANT LAM. The woman who had been attacking him was standing in front of Sergeant Lam, waving her arms dramatically.

"Your hand-to-hand combat is as good as mine," Teddy said, without thinking.

"You're a movie producer and I'm a secretary," the woman said, spinning toward Teddy, giving him a meaningful look. "I wouldn't say either of us should be good at hand-to-hand combat."

This woman clearly knew more about Teddy than he was comfortable with.

Sergeant Lam sighed and gripped the sides of his desk

tightly. Teddy watched the man's knuckles drain of color. When Sergeant Lam finally spoke, his words were precise.

"Fighting in the lounges is forbidden," Lam said.

Teddy cringed at the word *forbidden*. It sounded so dramatic and ridiculous. He just wanted to get back to L.A. and to the two lives he led that nowadays rarely involved hand-to-hand combat that wasn't staged.

"I'm sorry, sir. I haven't been sleeping well and my emotions got the better of me," Teddy said.

Sergeant Lam groaned but didn't say anything.

"I'm a movie producer," Teddy continued, "and I've been working on an action movie that has a lot of—"

"I don't care. Leave now. No more fighting."

Teddy didn't need to be told twice to leave and was out of the office and almost back to the lounge before he heard the woman yelling his name.

"Leave me alone," Teddy said.

"Peter Barrington sent me. He needs your help."

2

MILLIE MARTINDALE BOARDED A PLANE IN WASHINGTON, D.C., Thursday afternoon and was finally seeing the end of the trip more than twenty-four hours later as her CIA-chartered private plane landed in Macau. She sat at the back of the small plane. The rest of the seats were full of older white men representing both branches of Congress as well as the U.S. Department of Commerce and the U.S. Department of Justice. She took the final sip of her bottled water, poured the rest of her trail mix into her mouth, then followed the others off the plane.

They moved quickly to another area of the Macau Business Aviation Center where they watched a private jet larger than their own land. A man, who looked almost exactly like the other men in her group, stepped off and joined them in the waiting area. Arrow Donaldson was the head of a giant telecom conglomerate, as well as the owner of a professional basketball team in Los Angeles and a casino conglomerate in China.

The testimony was scheduled to be given at the U.S. Consulate General Hong Kong & Macau building, forty-five minutes away in Hong Kong, but their base of operations was in Macau due to unrest in Hong Kong. Millie also believed a big part of it was Arrow Donaldson wanting to show off the power and prestige he wielded in Macau. Arrow shook hands and patted backs with the government delegation, ignoring Millie.

Millie stuck out her hand and smiled pleasantly.

"I'm Millie Martindale. I work with Lance Cabot. He sent me to meet you."

"Where's Lance?" Arrow asked, not taking the hand Millie was offering.

Millie dropped her hand but kept her smile pasted in place, her eyes on Arrow.

"We've met before. I'm sure you don't remember, but I was the lead on the initiative at your casinos with the Chinese government officials," she said.

Arrow quickly moved in close to Millie, glaring at her.

"Shhhh. You never know who's listening around here."

"I know exactly who's listening. That's the point. I'm with the CIA."

"I only ever talked to Lance about what we were doing at the casino. He never mentioned you."

"Lance is the face of the operation, of course. He's the

director of the CIA. I'm the one who handles the details behind the scenes. Millie Martindale."

Millie had been working with Lance Cabot on a task force in one of Arrow's Chinese casinos to identify Chinese government workers with gambling problems and recruit them as U.S. spies. But Lance had reassigned her to this detail when Arrow approached Lance about bringing Li Feng to the U.S. to give testimony that could impact a new trade deal in the works between China and the U.S.

Li Feng was the chief financial officer and daughter of the founder of QuiTel, China's largest telecom company. QuiTel was suspected of using the cell phone equipment they sold in the U.S. to spy on U.S. citizens and was supposed to have been blacklisted from doing business in the country. But the suspicions were just that—suspicions, however well-founded. And without proof of wrongdoing, the company had been granted an exemption to that ban for several years. The exemption was due to expire at the end of the week, but China wanted the exemption for QuiTel to be made permanent as part of the new deal. If the CFO were to testify that the spying was real, it would squash the exemption for good.

Millie and Lance knew Arrow stood to benefit financially by selling new equipment to replace the cheaper equipment that QuiTel provided, but they suspected Arrow had other plans behind the scenes with more sinister potential. It was Millie's job to figure out what those plans were, and to stop them.

"I can't believe Lance pawned something this important off on a secretary."

This time Millie was the one who moved in closer to Arrow.

"I'm not a secretary, and I'm definitely not a pawn, Mr. Donaldson."

She put her hand out one more time, this time without a smile. Arrow shook it limply.

"You better watch your moves, Millie Martindale," Arrow said.

When Arrow walked away, Millie took a deep breath and exhaled. Lance had told her this would happen. Millie had been pushing Lance to give her more responsibility and this was the perfect chance. Arrow Donaldson had a reputation for having trouble dealing with people he believed were beneath him, especially women.

And if Arrow became angry or frustrated, he was bound to make a mistake, one that would let the CIA stop him before he did anything terrible. They had backup plans in place, of course, but Millie could already tell she was going to be able to crack Arrow Donaldson.

When her breathing returned to normal, Millie joined the rest of the group. Arrow was off to the side talking on his phone. He saw her watching him and she smiled. He put his phone in his suit coat pocket and came back toward the group.

"Li Feng will remain under my secure protection for another night," Arrow said. "So why don't you all head to your hotel to rest a bit and we'll regroup for dinner this evening?"

"That's not what we agreed to. That's not what *I* agreed to. I want to see Li Feng now."

"I just got off the phone with your boss and he agreed to it."

"You talked to Lance?"

But Arrow had already moved on to his waiting vehicle, as had the rest of her group. She pulled out her cell phone to call Lance and demand to know why he'd sold her out.

"Sorry to give you no warning, Millie," he said, when he came on the line. "I figured it would help our plan to throw him off-balance, and you needed to act unguardedly. He's agreed to meet you at his stadium in a few minutes to show you how powerful he is and what kind of protection he can offer. Let him spout off and feel like a big man and keep your mouth shut. Let him think you're a secretary who is no threat to him."

Millie grumbled an acceptance and hung up her phone.

3

LI FENG WAS SO CLOSE TO BEING ABLE TO RELAX. THE PLAN had seemed outlandish at first, and updates to it early on only made it seem more ludicrous. But here she was on her way to the airport to complete the last step in a plan that would give her what she wanted most in life and had never thought would be possible: freedom.

The first taste of freedom was being by herself in the car. For as long as she could remember, she'd always had a crowd of security personnel around her. As an adult, she understood why it was necessary, especially as her father grew his role in the Chinese government and left much of the running of QuiTel to her. The number of security personnel always seemed excessive to her, and she was certain that when she was younger the guards had been there more to spy on and control her than to protect her.

Even as she basked in the glorious freedom of the alone time she'd been given, all she could think about was Sonny Ma, the man who had shown her another life free of her parents and their influences and expectations, a life of excitement and fame and money not tied to her family or the Chinese government. They'd grown up together, both students at a school for the children of elite members of Chinese society, and both had dabbled in criminal activity out of boredom. While Li Feng's family had put an end to her "childish rebellions," Sonny Ma used his family resources and connections from the school to lay the foundation for a powerful criminal enterprise. Then he had dangled before Li Feng the possibility that she could be part of that exciting world, too.

But soon after showing her that life and letting the need for it infect her soul, he had ripped it away from her at her parents' command.

For that, Sonny Ma would pay dearly.

"The American producers have received the blackmail letter and their movie set has been attacked," Li Feng said to her driver. "You will do the rest. Soon everyone will believe Sonny Ma is back to his gangster ways, just as they're about to celebrate him with this ridiculous movie."

"Wouldn't it be easier to just kill him?"

"I will take his money, his reputation, and his freedom. He will *wish* he was dead. I will not grant him that mercy."

The little man driving the car was one more piece of the freedom she was being offered. Zhou "Ziggy" Peng was known around town as the most vicious fixer for Arrow Donaldson, the American billionaire with outsize influence in China due to his ownership of the largest and most profitable casino in Macau. He also owned the ferry that transported tourists between Hong Kong and Macau, as well as several high-profile government officials.

A year ago, Ziggy Peng showed up in her office to tell her that a number of her employees had high gambling debts and were likely in danger of being blackmailed. Little had she suspected at the time that this meeting would turn into the start of a new life for her. Days later, Ziggy returned with Arrow Donaldson, who told her about a plan he had in mind that would require her to lie to the U.S. government.

"What would it take for you to put yourself in that situation?" he had asked her.

"I want to destroy Sonny Ma."

Arrow gave her the use of Ziggy Peng and his resources, as well as arranging to get her a new identity—including all of the papers she would need to live in the U.S. and become rich and famous and free.

In exchange, all she had to do was tell some people from the U.S. government that her company was spying on U.S. citizens using the cellular equipment they sold to phone carriers, even though it wasn't true. That was the best part of the plan. Her testimony would ruin her family and taint her government. Her testimony was so prized that the U.S. government would bring in the CIA to protect her, which would also shield her from Sonny

Ma once he found out she was the one responsible for ruining his life.

As they approached the business aviation area of the airport, Ziggy Peng's phone rang. He nodded his head and said a few words acknowledging whatever was being said on the other line and then he hung up.

He turned back toward Li Feng and said, "There's been a change of plans. I'm taking you to your protected lodging instead of the airport."

4

"I'M DALE GAI," THE WOMAN SAID TO TEDDY.

"How do you know Peter Barrington?"

"I work for the resort where they're holding the film festival he's working with."

"I work with Peter as a producer, but I wasn't involved with the film festival business. I need to get back to L.A. and get some sleep."

"Peter needs you," Dale Gai said.

"You said that already, but I told you that I'm not working with him on the film festival."

"I'm an assistant in the security division of the resort. That's all I can tell you."

"Why didn't Peter just call me himself?"

"I volunteered to come for you. They don't know this

area like I do, and it would save time. Please. I can't say any more than that here."

Teddy considered the woman's hand-to-hand combat skills and wondered what kind of assistant she was.

"You were really just trying to wake me up?" he asked.

Dale nodded.

Peter didn't know the full extent of Teddy's life before becoming Billy Barnett—definitely not as much as his father, Stone Barrington, who had hunted Teddy *and* partnered with him—but he knew that Teddy had certain skills other producers didn't. Between the lack of sleep and the exhaustion from travel, he was beginning to feel more like a hard-luck tourist than a government-trained assassin and master of disguise. Had his career shifts toward movie producer and, more recently, stunt work and character acting ruined him for more dangerous work? He figured the easiest way to find out would be to follow this beautiful and mysterious woman.

"Okay. Let's go," Teddy said.

Dale led him to the SkyPier landing where they boarded a ferry for Macau. During the forty-five-minute ride across the South China Sea, Teddy spent significant time running through possible scenarios. Was he being set up? He thought about using his expert disguise skills and changing his appearance so he could ditch Dale Gai, but then he realized he'd left his luggage in the lounge at the airport, including his disguise and makeup kits.

"Are you okay?" Dale asked, with what seemed like genuine concern.

"I'm fine. It's just been a very long week, and I'm not as young as I used to be."

"None of us are."

"You managed to keep me from beating you to death when you surprised me in my sleep, so you're doing something right," Teddy said.

"Ten years ago, it wouldn't have taken me that long to beat you."

"Ten years ago, I wouldn't have fallen asleep in an airport," Teddy said.

Dale laughed and Teddy felt better about the situation.

"Now that we're out of the airport, can you tell me more about what's happening with Peter? Is Ben Bacchetti with him still? Are they safe? Have you called Ben's dad? Where's Stone Barrington?"

Dale paused, and then said, "The man who owns the casino and resort complex where they're having the Macau Film Festival is the same man who owns this ferry company. Who would have thought that an American could have that much sway in our part of the world?"

"What man is that?"

"His name is Arrow Donaldson. It's been a long day and I don't really feel like talking anymore."

Teddy may have been a step behind in close combat, but he didn't need to be told twice that Dale was offering a number of red flags in her speech. Wherever they went, someone was listening.

5

THE GOLDEN DESERT CASINO AND RESORT LOOKED LIKE A stack of giant cargo boxes that had been designed by an abstract artist, painted in metallic pastels, and dumped in the middle of the Cotai Strip's more traditionally garish luxury hotels and resorts. It was one of the ugliest things Teddy had ever seen, and he had been a lot of places and seen a lot of ugly things.

"Why does it look like that?" Teddy asked Dale Gai.

"The architect owed the government much money and agreed to do upgrades to the casino for free to help pay back the debt. Everyone assumes it was a terrible joke he played on the government that they didn't get."

"Why would the government give money to remodel a casino owned by an American billionaire?" Teddy asked.

"The casinos are the shining stars of Macau. How they look and how much money they make reflects on the government here, good or bad."

"And the Golden Desert was reflecting badly?"

"No, nothing like that. The Golden Desert is the brightest of the shining stars. But they wanted it to be even bigger and more elaborate."

"And Arrow Donaldson went along with it?"

"Arrow Donaldson didn't have a choice."

Dale led Teddy through the lobby of the hotel and up to the top level of the largest of the gaudy storage crates, where the security offices were housed in a spartanly furnished office suite full of uniformed security officers working on computers. Along one wall was a massive array of security monitors.

Stone Barrington stood in the middle of the room. When he saw Teddy and Dale approaching, he came over to greet them, then led them to a luxurious conference room with plush carpet and warm wood tones and, more importantly, generous glasses of cool whiskey. Dino Bacchetti, the police commissioner of New York City, Peter Barrington, and Ben Bacchetti were already seated at the table.

Stone thanked Dale. Dale smiled, nodded, then left the room. When the door was closed, Stone took a seat at the head of the table and picked up a remote control in front of him and played a video.

When the video was over, Teddy said, "Again. From the beginning."

The video scurried backward before starting again. Nothing changed.

Finally, Teddy looked away from the screen and turned his attention to Peter and Ben.

"It looks real, doesn't it?" Dino said. "If I hadn't been sitting across from the both of them when this was supposed to be happening, I would be sending them off to jail myself."

"It's just so obvious," Stone said.

Teddy nodded and looked back at the video monitors. Ostensibly it showed Stone Barrington's son, Peter, and Dino's son, Ben, at a high-limit poker table. The two men were cheating, and not subtly—pulling chips off the table when it looked like their bets were going to go bad and adding chips when their bets paid off.

The time stamp on the video was from two days ago. Peter, Ben, and Stone were all in town for the Macau Film Festival. China was the biggest market for U.S. films and, in particular, for Centurion Studios, where Peter was a director, Ben was the president, and Stone was a majority investor.

Macau was far behind the mainland China and Hong Kong film industries and didn't have any formalized film schools or training programs. Seeking to expand Centurion's share in the crowded Chinese market, Peter and Ben were part of a program to share their expertise in exchange for priority influence with their films.

"What do the security people here say?" Teddy asked. "Casino security bosses don't normally let a bunch of folks sit in their camera vault unattended, especially not Chinese security bosses and American visitors."

"Never could put one past you, could I?" Stone stood up and put his hand on Teddy's shoulder. "I've worked with the head of gaming security in Macau before on a sensitive matter, so he owed me a favor."

"This isn't just about the video, is it?" Teddy asked.

"A few days before we found out about the video, we received this at our production office," Ben said. He handed Teddy a typewritten letter demanding they hire the Solid Gold triad to provide security for the set or suffer further attacks.

"'Further attacks'?" Teddy asked. "There have been other attacks?"

"They were small things that we didn't even think about at the time," Ben said. "Like, kids throwing rocks at the set and some punks on motorcycles driving by and threatening us. We just assumed it was locals hazing the foreigners."

"But then this big guy showed up one day and ripped the air conditioner right out of our production building and ran off with it," Peter said. "The next day we received the letter, and we went to the film festival organizers to ask for their help. They assigned us Dale Gai for protection, and to serve as liaison to the security team for the casino and the festival."

"So it's a good, old-fashioned protection racket," Teddy said.

"With a new, high-tech twist," Dino said.

Stone downloaded the security footage to a thumb

drive for Teddy and told him they were heading back to the U.S. that night.

"The festival is almost over, and this is too much. But I want you to stay behind and find whoever is responsible. They tried to make our sons appear to be criminals."

6

WHILE STONE BARRINGTON WENT WITH DINO, PETER, AND Ben to have a final round of drinks with the film festival executives, he let Teddy use his suite at the Golden Desert. Teddy removed his watch and popped off a small magnetic disc that he attached to the back of the hotel phone. With the signal now scrambled, he called the basement of a home in Washington, D.C.

"It's me," Teddy said when Kevin Cushman, aka Warplord924, answered.

"Last time you said, 'Do you know who this is?'" Kevin said.

"Last time I wasn't in a hurry."

"I like being in a hurry. It usually means fun trouble."

Kevin Cushman lived with his mother and appeared on the surface to embody all of the characteristics of a lazy video-game-addicted man-baby. But underneath the layers of vintage T-shirts and nacho cheese dust was a man who made six figures as a computer security analyst and had done some covert and tricky work for Teddy in the past.

"I'm sending you a video. I need to know everything about it."

"Video is new for you," Kevin said.

"Nothing is new for me, but this is the first time I've had one I thought you could help with."

"You don't think I'm good enough to help you with other videos?"

"Believe it or not, people used to pride themselves in doing things for themselves."

Kevin snorted.

"So you can help with video?"

"I mean, unless you're about to put an old VCR tape in an envelope and mail it to me, I can help."

"Why would I send you a VCR tape?" Teddy asked.

"Analog is all the rage now. Videotapes, vinyl records, paper books. All that stuff is making a comeback."

Teddy ignored Kevin and opened a laptop Stone had left behind for him that had an encryption program on it that Teddy had designed himself, with some help from Kevin. He plugged in the thumb drive Ben had given him, ran the video through the encryption program, and then sent it to Kevin.

"Sent," Teddy said. "You know how to get ahold of me."

7

STONE BARRINGTON RETURNED FROM DRINKS WHILE TEDDY was still in his suite waiting for Kevin Cushman to call him back. The TV was turned to an international version of CNN and a bucket of ice was melting on the table next to the television. Teddy had his shoes off and was lying on the largest couch in the suite, about to fall asleep again, when Stone entered.

"I can come back when you've left if you need the place to yourself," Teddy said, not moving from his position on the couch.

"Nonsense," Stone said. "Were you having a drink with that melting ice or using it to nurse that knot on your head?"

"What knot on my head?"

Teddy put his hand up instinctively to his forehead and felt around until he hit a small soft patch that made him flinch when he touched it. He got off the couch and went into the bathroom to look at himself in the mirror.

"Did you fall off the bed when you were napping?" Stone asked.

"I wasn't napping. I think that woman did this to me."

Stone smiled widely.

"A woman. I see. So definitely no napping. Just bruising?"

"I wasn't going to bed with her. It was Dale Gai. The woman Peter sent to come and find me in Hong Kong."

"Why wouldn't you go to bed with Dale Gai, if she were interested? There is nothing about her looks that would make any natural man turn away from her advances."

"It's not her looks that concern me, but her skills. I was sleeping in the airport lounge and she attacked me. Now it looks like she left a mark."

Teddy could feel a ball of anger rising in his chest, but he couldn't figure out why. This wasn't the first time he'd been attacked, not even the first time he'd been attacked by a woman. And it did seem like it was all a misunderstanding. Still, he felt uncomfortable at how she had found his weak spots. And in his sleep-deprived state, Teddy didn't like feeling uncomfortable.

"Are you okay?" Stone asked when Teddy started to wobble.

"Fine," Teddy said. "I just need sleep."

"I can't offer sleep, but the drinks at the film festival

lounge were terrible and I think we could both use a good steak to go with them."

As Stone talked, there was a knock on the door and then Dino Bacchetti entered.

"There's a party in our room and nobody invited me," Dino said.

"No party, just some melting ice and a bruised movie producer," Stone said.

Dino looked at the bruise on Teddy's head and winced. "You run into a wall or something?"

"Dale Gai punched him while he was sleeping in an airport lounge in Hong Kong," Stone said.

"Is that some kind of new kinky thing I'm too old to know about?" Dino asked.

"It was just a misunderstanding."

"We were going to go for steaks and real drinks," Stone said.

"Now that sounds like a party," Dino said.

♦ ♦ ♦

The Oasis Grill sat at the top of the Golden Desert Casino and had dazzling views of the Cotai Strip, Macau's newest strip of glittering casinos and resort hotels, which was the city's latest attempt to turn Macau into a larger, richer copy of Las Vegas. The hotels along the strip were all owned by foreign investors, from the U.S. and Europe mostly, and included names familiar in Vegas like Sands, Caesars, and Wynn.

Teddy, Stone, and Dino ordered porterhouse steaks

aged in Himalayan salt, along with doubles of Knob Creek and talked about the video and the blackmail letter. Dino was still fuming about it.

"It'll be taken care of," Stone said, waving with his drink hand in Teddy's direction.

"I'll call Millie Martindale," Teddy said. "She's been working with Lance Cabot on and off at the CIA. She might know more about this."

"We know the video is fake, and doesn't reflect what was actually happening at the time. Which means anybody who was watching the live security feed wouldn't have seen anything out of the ordinary."

"I'll talk to casino security as well and see if there's anything else they forgot to tell us."

"Did Peter or Ben mention anything else?"

"They don't run into this stuff in the U.S.," Dino said. "We haven't had gang activities on movie sets for decades."

"There does seem to be an outlaw atmosphere here that's probably too raw for good guys like Peter and Ben," Teddy said.

"They just came over to help, and look what happened. No good deed goes unpunished, I guess," Dino said.

Stone waved his hands to try and shut down the conversation.

"There's no sense in being sad and gloomy. Our plane leaves in a few hours and our friend Teddy here will stay behind to find out what happened and make sure anyone responsible gets what's coming to them."

"You know who I am and what I do," Teddy said. "Once I start, I'm not going to stop until I finish it my way."

"We'll have a drink waiting for you when you return. And maybe after this you can find a woman to pal around with who doesn't leave you bruised."

8

WHEN THE STEAKS WERE GONE AND THE LAST ROUND OF Knob Creek finished, Stone and Dino decided against dessert. Stone called his driver to take them to the airport early, leaving Teddy by himself. He went back to the suite and saw a note from Stone on the coffee table letting him know that a friend had called about a movie and that Teddy would know how to get ahold of him.

"Me again," Teddy said when Kevin answered.

"I'd love to ask about where you are and what you're doing there, but even secure lines like this can have extra ears, so I'll keep my opinions to myself."

"Not your opinions about the video I sent, though," Teddy said.

"These aren't opinions. These are facts."

"I appreciate your confidence in your abilities and knowledge."

"What you sent me is something they call a deepfake video," Kevin said.

"It looked very real to me and everyone who saw it," Teddy said.

"That's the 'deep' part of deepfake."

"How do they create them? Is it animation? Artificial intelligence?"

"I'm not a video guy. I don't know the hows and such of these things, but my sense is that most of it is composed of real video and then certain key elements, like faces, are replaced."

"Like special effects in movies?" Teddy asked.

"Exactly. Until recently they've mostly been used to put famous actresses' faces on other women's bodies in adult movies, but now the bad guys are looking for ways to use them to bring down governments."

"Can you tell me who made it?"

"Eventually."

"I don't have time for eventually. Eventually I can find out on my own. I call you when I need things right now."

"I didn't know that speed was the only thing I brought to the table," Kevin said.

"Oh for crying out loud," Teddy said.

"Sometimes you can't rush quality."

Teddy bit his tongue. He was confident he could find out what he needed without Kevin's help, but it would take longer than Teddy was comfortable with, especially trying to do it in a foreign country he hadn't been to for many years.

"I haven't slept in a very long time. I apologize if I was harsh," Teddy said.

"Why haven't you been sleeping? Do you have insomnia?"

"I've been traveling a lot for work across different time zones and I keep getting called back into action. I'll be fine and you'll be fine. Just call me when you have more information on the video."

"Fine."

"Hey, if you didn't have any answers then why'd you call?"

"To tell you that what you have is a deepfake video," Kevin said.

"That's it?"

"That's *huge*. A video like this one isn't just a goof cooked up by kids in a garage. It's a big deal."

"Okay," Teddy said.

"There are only a few people who can do this kind of stuff with this level of realism, and they don't ever do it for fun. They do it to cause massive harm. I'll call back when I know more."

9

WHEN HE GOT OFF THE PHONE WITH KEVIN CUSHMAN, Teddy went back to the couch in the suite and sat down. He wanted to lie down and get some sleep so he was fresh for what needed to be done, but he couldn't get Kevin's warning out of his head. Teddy had assumed the video was an elaborate prank to go along with the typed note looking for protection money.

Protection rackets had long been a popular fundraising activity for low-level gangs, who'd blackmail business owners into paying money to protect themselves from attacks by the gang itself. But low-level gangs didn't have the technological savvy to pull off something this complex, which made Teddy wonder what else was going on. What had Peter and Ben gotten themselves involved in?

Someone had specifically targeted them and had gone

to the trouble to create this fake video that painted them as criminals. Even though people close to Peter and Ben knew the video was fake, it was so realistic that anyone else would have to doubt their innocence. Which made Teddy wonder if maybe Peter's and Ben's fathers were the true targets. Stone and Dino had collected enough enemies between them to fill out a rogues' gallery—Teddy had been one of those enemies for a while—and both of them had built up impressive security networks to protect themselves. But maybe someone had seen Peter and Ben as easier targets with the same payoff of hurting Stone or Dino.

Teddy was upset he hadn't had this information at dinner and found himself getting irrationally angry at Kevin again. He really needed to get some sleep before he either said something that would get him in trouble or ran into someone with Dale Gai's skill set who really *was* intent on hurting him.

10

THE DRIVER STOPPED AT THE GATE AND WOULDN'T TAKE Millie any closer to the site because he said he didn't have the right clearances. Millie suspected he was just being a jerk. Millie got out of the SUV, crawled under the gate, and took a few steps toward the construction site before turning back to see the SUV backing out of the drive and heading back toward the hotel. She sighed, then swore under her breath before walking the rest of the way to the heart of the site.

The stadium and field area were still under construction, but the attached building where the restaurants and suites would be housed was close to completion. Millie wandered the site, looking for a way into the finished part of the building. Eventually she found her way to an elevator that not only worked but went right to the top of the building and opened up on the owner's suite where Arrow Donaldson was staring out at his city under construction.

"I guess you *are* more than a secretary," Arrow said, bemused, when he turned to see Millie standing in his suite. "Did you walk all the way up here through the construction?"

"A flimsy gate and some scaffolding aren't going to stop the CIA, Mr. Donaldson."

"The CIA should have that carved into their headquarters, like the line about rain and snow for the post office."

"Did you know that line isn't even about the U.S. Postal Service?" Millie said.

"Oh really?"

"There is no official USPS motto. That line was paraphrased from a book about the Persian Wars that one of the architects of the post office in New York City read. It was about the Persian postal workers."

"I bet you've had that in your back pocket for a while just waiting to use it on someone, haven't you?"

"I'm in the intelligence service, Mr. Donaldson—I pick up a lot of information I find useful and interesting. Some of it has a natural place in conversation and the rest I keep to myself for my own purposes. But I never save anything just to use it to impress anyone."

"I never said I was impressed," Arrow said.

"Where's Li Feng?"

"She's safe."

Millie walked closer to Arrow. She was stunned by

how beautiful the area looked from where they were standing. Even more impressive than the actual view was the power that the view reflected. She felt like she was looking across the city as a god watching her subjects. That likely wasn't a coincidence. As she turned to look at Arrow, she could see him basking in the power of the view as well. She cleared her head and turned her focus to the task at hand. She didn't want to be seduced by the view or by Arrow's facade.

"Li Feng isn't your charge to protect," Millie said.

"People have this idea of billionaires as disconnected from reality, hiring people to do everything for them while they hide out in their billionaire bubbles unaware of how the real world works. But that's not me."

Millie noticed he managed to mention two separate times that he was a billionaire in one sentence.

"Good for you. But Li Feng is a government witness to corruption and espionage, and I've been charged with her protection."

Arrow gestured at the building they were standing in, at the window and its majestic view. "All of this is because of me. I made this happen and, despite what you may believe, I'm not taking a dime of government subsidies to do it. I have faith that this will be a success and I don't like to hedge my bets when I'm confident in something."

"Confidence is not a valid substitute for protection, Mr. Donaldson."

"Call me Arrow. Please."

"Last names are fine. And I do respect your ability to

make things happen. But I wouldn't be very good at my job if I let someone else swoop in and take it from me just because he has a lot of money."

"I made this happen. Aren't you listening to me? Without me, you wouldn't have a job to do."

"I don't see what a basketball stadium has to do with protecting a government witness."

"I am the *only* American to ever build a stadium on Chinese soil. Do you realize the kind of power that takes? The kind of respect I am afforded? Meanwhile, the U.S. government can't even stop China from spying on them. Li Feng is safer with me."

Millie took a few more steps toward Arrow. She could see his posture change and she knew the closer she got, the more uncomfortable he was.

"That really is very impressive, all of it. But I know how it was really built, and I know who else was involved."

"Pardon?"

"I told you I was Lance's point person for the initiative at your casino with the CIA."

"Where are you going with this *Ms.* Martindale?"

"Intelligence gathering is information gathering, and I'm very good at my intelligence job, which means I have a lot of information."

She took two more steps. Arrow backed away.

"Okay."

"I know *everything*."

Arrow turned away from Millie and took three large steps toward the bar cart in the center of the suite. He poured a generous amount of amber liquor from a crystal decanter into a crystal tumbler that glistened as he moved it in his hand. He took a long drink, then turned back to face Millie.

"Let Li Feng get settled with me tonight with some creature comforts. Then if you give me a call tomorrow, I can arrange for her to be transferred to your care."

Millie nodded. She liked Arrow feeling as if he was doing her a favor.

"Thank you. I can show myself out."

11

TEDDY GAVE UP TRYING TO NAP AND DRANK ALL THE COF-fee he could find in the suite instead. By the time Kevin Cushman called him back he felt great.

"I had to hack a Chinese government computer to get this. That was a first," Kevin said.

"I'd really prefer not to hear about how you do what you do."

"No. Right. I get it. That was just pretty cool. It was the first time I got to do that."

"About the video," Teddy said.

"Right. It's definitely a fake also. And it turns out that both fakes bear the signatures of Bing-Wen Jo. His nickname is Bingo."

"Like the dog?"

"Or the parlor game popular with older Americans.

From what I can find, he started out creating fake adult movie clips, then rode the technology wave enough to make millions of dollars. When he discovered a way to make instant fake videos using video clips and photos, he thought it was going to be his big break."

"I'm guessing his big break never showed up."

"The Chinese government keeps quite a file on this guy, and it seems to indicate Bing-Wen Jo is as good at violence as he is with computers. HR records show Arrow Donaldson officially hired him for the security team at his casino, but online chatter and rumors suspect his real job is secretly helping Arrow with off-the-books projects."

"Dale Gai told me about Arrow Donaldson. I'll have to see what else she can tell me about him and Bingo."

"Donaldson is a major Republican backer and likes to fund congressional candidates and presidential candidates who like to talk tough against China."

Teddy saw the bigger picture. "He props up politicians who play the bad cop, so he can come in and act like the good cop and use his government connections to push things through. This is helpful. Thank you."

"One other thing. I had to dig through a few complex identity layers to find the signatures that linked to Bing-Wen Jo. Anyone else looking at this would trace it back to a Chinese gangster named Sonny Ma."

Teddy hung up and scratched the side of his head. This wasn't great news, but it was more information than he'd had before. He'd long ago learned to appreciate having as much information as possible, even if it turned out to be hard information to swallow.

He still worried he had offended Kevin Cushman and wondered if there was a way to show his thanks without being over the top. He went back to his laptop and logged into one of his many bank accounts and bought a substantial amount of in-game currency for an online game that he knew Kevin liked to play, and transferred it to a profile he knew Kevin liked to use.

A few minutes later Teddy a got a text message on his phone from a number he didn't recognize and suspected didn't even really exist. It was a picture of a hand making a thumbs-up gesture. He knew it was from Kevin and he smiled.

While he had his phone in his hand, he decided to make another call to someone else who'd done him a number of favors over the years. Millie Martindale had started as an assistant to the president's national security adviser and managed to use her intelligence, her looks, and a special dogged charm to work her way into a series of escalating positions of influence and action. Recently Teddy had used her to keep in touch with Lance Cabot while Teddy was undercover in Paris. Millie had sprouted roots in Lance's office since then, and was making quite a name for herself.

"Hello," Millie said.

"Me again," Teddy said.

"I still don't know your name."

"I don't believe that, but I appreciate you being discreet."

"Who do I get to be a go-between with this time?"

"Nobody. I just need information."

"How boring."

"It's not all international subterfuge and murdered terrorists."

"You murdered the terrorist," Millie said.

"And you took credit for it."

"Not by choice."

"You've been working with Lance Cabot lately, right?"

"Yes . . ."

"Do you know what Lance and the CIA might be doing with casinos and Chinese gangsters?"

"You're not the only one I'm discreet with."

"I can just hack into the CIA network again like I always do and find out myself. I just wanted to give you a chance to pay me back the favor for putting you in Lance's office."

"You can try to hack into the network. Keeping you out of it is one of the things he put me in charge of."

"He got tired of trying to keep a dead man out of his computers?"

"Sorry. I have to go. Enjoy Macau."

Millie hung up before Teddy could ask her how she knew he was in Macau.

12

AS TEDDY WANDERED AROUND THE SUITE WONDERING what to do with the information he had gotten from Kevin, he noticed a pile of cases and bags just inside the doorway. Since Teddy had left his luggage in the Hong Kong airport lounge, Peter had said he'd gather some stuff from the film set to tide Teddy over. Peter and Teddy both knew it wasn't clothes he'd been missing from his luggage. He quickly found the smallest bag and took it into the bathroom where he unlocked it and unpacked a small cache of makeup and effects material. It wasn't a great disguise kit, but it was enough for what Teddy needed to do.

Teddy had disguised himself as people ranging from a cabdriver to a professional athlete, but there was one disguise he'd long wanted to try but never had the opportunity. It was his biggest challenge and his most taboo subject. He worked as quickly as possible while still getting the details right. When he finally finished, he looked in the mirror and a completely different man was looking back at him.

Stone Barrington.

Teddy left the suite and made the rounds of the casino in his Stone Barrington disguise. He would be convincing on video, but anyone who knew Stone would never buy it in person, so Teddy was guarded with his movements. Stone Barrington was a memorable man, so there was no telling how many people he had made an impression on during his short time in Macau.

He wanted to meet with Zhou Peng, the head of casino security and, Teddy suspected, one of Arrow Donaldson's right-hand men, but first he wanted to establish video evidence of Stone's appearance in the casino after he'd allegedly left town. When Teddy was convinced he'd created enough of a video trail, he headed up to the security office.

Dale Gai was the first person who met him in the office. She was pleasant and feigned acceptance of Teddy's disguise, but he could tell she knew something was wrong.

"I'd like to speak to Zhou Peng," Teddy said, in his most booming Stone-like voice.

"You shouldn't be here."

"My work usually takes me places where I should not be. It's the nature of my business."

"And what would that business be, Mr. Barrington?"

"Ah, so you remember me."

"I know *exactly* who you are," she said. "Zhou Peng is away from the office right now, escorting a high-profile guest to a more secure location."

Teddy knew right away that Dale was giving him a thinly veiled clue that Zhou Peng was more than the head of casino security, and that Teddy should proceed carefully.

Zhou Peng interrupted them, and he didn't seem happy to see Stone.

"I understand that this is awkward," Teddy said. "I want to help find whoever is responsible for trying to frame or blackmail my son."

"There is nothing you can do right now to help your son, Mr. Barrington," Peng said. "If I can be of assistance making other arrangements for you to talk with other people, I would be most happy."

"Have you had any other problems with fake videos on your security cameras?"

"I have received no confirmation that there have been *any* fake videos on my security cameras. Thank you."

"Okay, thank you for your time. Just one more question. Do you know a man named Bing-Wen Jo?"

Teddy could tell immediately he'd hit a nerve when Zhou's eyes turned to small pinpricks and a flush of red washed across his face. It was quick, but it was all Teddy needed. On his way out of the office, he stopped by Dale Gai's desk.

"When are you off work?"

"I don't socialize with visitors to the casino, Mr. *Barrington.*"

She said the name overly dramatically, and Teddy wasn't sure if it was helping or hurting his cause.

"I have no trouble filling my social calendar. What I could use more of are your tips on how to navigate this complicated environment."

"You flatter me. I'm sure your business has taken you into far more complicated environments than our casino."

"Now you're the one offering flattery."

She took a second to breathe, then looked to her left as Zhou Peng wove his way through the floor of the security office. Peng made eye contact with Teddy, then with Dale. His gaze lingered on both of them a few seconds too long for Teddy's comfort, but eventually he waved for Dale to follow him and then walked away.

"Room 5318," Dale said. "Why don't you change into something that's more *you* and meet me in thirty minutes?"

"I'll make myself comfortable if you do the same."

"Thirty minutes."

She nodded softly and went to meet Peng in his office.

◆ ◆ ◆

"Why is Stone Barrington still in my hotel?" Peng asked. "What did you tell him? What did he ask you?"

"He wanted to talk to you. I told him you were busy and that he should let you do your job."

"Why is he still in the casino? I thought he left. His plane left. Why is he still here?"

"Are you sure it was his plane?"

Peng's face went bright red and his eyes exploded with rage. He swiped his hand across the desk and caught hold of a thick golden apple. His fingers wrapped around the apple and his swipe turned to a throw. The apple soared across the room and hit Dale Gai under her right cheek. She crumpled to the ground and Peng rushed to stand over her.

"Is that a satisfying answer to your question? Does it inspire you to ask more questions?"

"No. Thank you."

He continued looking down at her as she squirmed and held her cheek but didn't cry or scream.

"Perhaps you should take the rest of the day off to think about your role in this organization."

Dale nodded and bit her lip, then turned and left.

Peng's eyes followed her as she departed. The woman was going to be a problem.

13

ARROW DONALDSON WATCHED FROM HIS SUITE IN THE STA- dium as the girl from the CIA made her way back through the construction site and to the SUV that had returned for her. He knew it was a risk rushing away from the airport as quickly as he had because it made him look suspicious. He'd been counting on Lance Cabot and the rest of the government delegation to give him the free rein he was accustomed to in his city, but this girl was going to be trouble. His initial burst of surprise and admiration for her moxie had faded, replaced by resentment and fear that she would ruin his carefully calibrated plan.

When the girl's SUV pulled away, Arrow dialed every number he had for Lance Cabot and got a series of voice-mails, anonymous beeps, and even a busy signal before he stopped trying. Instead, he called a local number and spoke to Ziggy Peng.

"Change of plans," Arrow said.

"It's always change of plans with you. Why even plan?"

"I've attained my position by being nimble when necessary. If my methods bother you, you are more than free to seek employment elsewhere."

"What is the change?"

"I need you to do the job tonight instead of tomorrow."

"It will be handled."

"Let me know when it's done."

"Of course."

"Oh, one more thing," Arrow said.

"Yes. There's always one more thing."

"There will be another woman there, an American with the CIA. If she dies as well, there will be bonuses for everyone."

♦ ♦ ♦

Ziggy Peng hung up the phone and sat down behind his desk, twirling in his chair like a child. He wasn't happy with how he'd handled Dale Gai. It was never right to hit a woman, even if it had the desired effect. He picked up the golden apple he'd thrown at Dale and took a bite. No sense in it going to waste.

The plan had always called for an attack on the visitors from the United States government and the traitor Li

Feng, and the specifics of the plan came together easily. The Chinese military had lately been testing stealth drones in Macau and Hong Kong. They were small and easy to maneuver, but also had enough firepower and kill capabilities to rival a small fighter jet. Bingo, with his technological expertise, was going to hijack one.

Finding a drone to hijack had been easy. U.S. tech companies had found numerous weaknesses in the drones' security, and a few rebellious souls had posted on message boards tips for hacking them in an attempt to make themselves feel better about conspiring with the Chinese government to spy on dissenters. The more complicated part of the plan was developing programming code that would hide the true origin of the hack and make it look as though a former gangster from Macau named Sonny Ma was responsible. Ziggy Peng found the whole thing ridiculous.

He'd tried many times to convince Li Feng that elaborate plans were always a terrible idea and that if she hated a man, she should kill him. Ziggy Peng had killed many men that he hated, and many more that other men hated. This was the first time he'd been involved in an intricate plot just to make a man look foolish. Men rarely needed help looking foolish.

"Are you ready?" Ziggy asked Bingo when he answered.

"For which part?"

"For all parts. You need to go tonight. Soon."

"I'll be ready." Bingo hung up.

With the key part of that plan in motion, Ziggy turned his mind to the problem of Dale Gai.

♦ ♦ ♦

Arrow Donaldson was in the back of his SUV when Ziggy Peng called to tell him they were a go. When they hung up, Arrow called Millie Martindale.

"I'm still very impressed at your initiative and stubbornness," Arrow said.

"That's very nice of you to say, even if it's a lie," Millie said.

Arrow clenched his teeth and took a pause so he didn't say something that would put the whole plan in jeopardy. He'd had enough of this woman's second-guessing and impertinence. A man in his position had earned deference. Was owed it. Why was that so hard?

"Take it however you will," Arrow finally said, "but the truth is that you made your case and I don't see any reason not to put Li Feng in your care as soon as possible."

"Really?"

Her tone was more suspicious than thankful, but he held his temper in check. He wasn't an impulsive man, and the reason he'd made it as far as he had—and was able to get people to do his bidding—was because he didn't fly off the handle like he'd seen other men in charge do. A response to a challenge should always be calculated.

"I have other things to attend to. This city is very important to me, and I am very important to this city."

"Yes, I understand," Millie said, her tone once again implying doubt.

Arrow felt a flare of anger, and reminded himself that Millie Martindale would soon no longer be a thorn in his side. He gave her the address of a hotel on the water and the room number where she was to go and hung up before she could say anything further.

14

ROOM 3347 AT THE GOLDEN DESERT CASINO AND RESORT was packed with CIA protective agents on loan from the local Agency field office, room service staff, three of the U.S. government delegates, and Millie Martindale. She wasn't sure how her room had become the operations center for everything, but as she hung up with Arrow Donaldson, she was happy they were all together. Millie banged on a room service platter until everyone in the room was quiet.

"We have a change in plans. We're getting Li Feng out tonight. Right now."

"This feels more like a kidnapping exchange than a transfer of custody," one of the agents said.

"I don't trust this guy any more than I trust a kidnapper," Millie said. "Maybe even less."

"Then why are we doing this? Why are we negotiating with a private citizen for a government asset?"

"This is a complicated situation with multiple stakeholders, private and governmental," Millie said. "Your job is to follow my directions."

Another agent joined them, and then two more. All men.

"What if you're sending us into a trap?" another one of the agents asked. He was the tallest man in the room, and he loomed over Millie.

"We are men and women of the CIA," Millie said, squawking a bit at first, but finding the depth in her voice quickly. "Every room we go into could be a trap. Every restaurant, every drive, every phone call could be our last. If you want a safe job and a boring life, go work for Treasury."

Millie stood on the balls of her feet as she finished, partially to compensate for the male agent's height, but also because she was energized and excited after her speech. Perhaps, naïvely, she expected the speech to be enough that the rest of the group would fall into line and head out, even if they didn't cheer out loud for her. But nobody moved and everyone in the room continued staring at her.

"You're the only woman here," the first agent she'd been talking to said.

"What if the person we're going to rescue doesn't need to be saved?" another agent asked.

The tall one kept looking at her with a crooked smile, and she hoped he was about to say something to galvanize the crew to her side. Instead, he said, "Treasury took down Al Capone."

Millie was spared further embarrassment when the phone in her room rang. She pushed through the group of men to get to it.

"I own a high-rise of beautiful condos near the site where I'm building my arena," Arrow said.

"Are they as beautiful as the casino you built?"

Millie could hear Arrow sigh on the other end of the line.

"Li Feng is in the penthouse expecting your visit."

"I'm on my way over there right now," Millie said.

"I know you want to protect her, but maybe don't take an entire army over there. She's used to a certain level of luxury and discretion. I fear your goon squad dressed like an assault team might do more harm than good."

"I hate to admit it, but you might have a point."

Millie hung up and looked around at the men in the room. Almost all of them were dressed in military gear, including all three who'd been taunting her. Three others, though, would work. One was wearing casual office attire and could have come from an IT department, and the other two were dressed in blazers, dress shirts, and dress pants. She pointed to the three of them and told them to follow her.

"The rest of you stay here and make sure no one steals anything from the minibar."

15

BINGO HAD FINISHED THE CODE FOR THE DRONE HACK WELL before Ziggy Peng called, but he'd hoped to fine-tune it more before go-time. That wasn't going to happen now. He only had a few minutes to finish processing everything and track down the drone he was going to use.

The plan had been much easier during the initial stages, because the Chinese government had been testing stealth drones throughout the country, including heavily in the special administrative regions of Hong Kong and Macau. But the recent unrest and protests in Hong Kong had diverted the government's attention, and most of the drones had been sent to Hong Kong, leaving only a couple in Macau.

Ziggy Peng called again. "They are going to be in the penthouse of the building we discussed. It's a circular suite with windows on all sides, so targeting shouldn't be a problem."

"All of those fancy buildings have window coverings. It won't stop a bullet, but it will make it hard to see who I'm shooting."

"It's all controlled electronically. I trust you're able to hack something as simple as window shades."

Electric shades were as easy as anything in a house to hack, but it added another task to an already tight time frame. But knowing his protests would fall on deaf ears, Bingo said nothing.

Perhaps sensing Bingo's silent discontent, Ziggy spoke again with a more pleasant tone.

"Arrow Donaldson has talked the female agent into taking a smaller group of agents with her."

This was not the type of good news Bingo had been expecting. Ziggy continued talking.

"If the American woman is killed during the attack, Arrow Donaldson has promised bonuses for all involved."

"Then she will die."

♦ ♦ ♦

Millie pulled up to the high-rise to which Arrow had directed her, located at the end of the strip near the more naturalistic area of Coloane Village. The exterior looked to be made entirely of windows so that every unit boasted an uninterrupted grand view, one of the many luxuries the building afforded.

The men she'd brought with her were quiet and deferential, but she knew they were capable of taking on anything they faced on their way up to the penthouse. As Millie conversed with the driver of the SUV about where to park to make sure they could get in and out as quickly as possible, the other three agents went around to the back of the SUV. Two of them grabbed assault rifles, and the other grabbed a shotgun. Millie also took a shotgun, and the four of them entered the building. Obviously having been appraised of their imminent arrival, the guard at the desk waved the party through and gave Millie the code for the elevator to access the penthouse.

"Mr. Donaldson says hello," the guard said.

"I'm sure he does," Millie said.

She knew it was not a casual greeting, but rather one more way for Arrow Donaldson to show her he was watching.

The elevator zipped Millie and her team quickly to the top of the building, and as they exited onto the penthouse floor, Millie suddenly felt very vulnerable. The walls were all glass. While others might find the views awe-inspiring, Millie merely felt exposed.

Millie hurried everyone off the elevator and toward the entrance of the penthouse. Li Feng answered on the second knock and Millie pushed everyone quickly inside. She was pleased to find that the apartment had dark drapes pulled down over all the windows. Li Feng was dressed in the same long, dark coat and dark hat and sunglasses she'd been wearing when she had been whisked away by Arrow right after her arrival. Millie let her breath return to normal speed and she relaxed her muscles. Maybe, for once, something would go as smoothly as planned.

♦ ♦ ♦

While Li Feng gathered her luggage, the agent in the polo shirt came over to Millie with a concerned look on his face.

"This doesn't feel right," he said, looking back toward the bedroom where Li Feng was visible in the doorway. After briefly greeting her CIA protectors, the soft-spoken woman had told them she'd be ready in a few minutes, and asked them to be seated while she finished getting ready. None of them took her up on the offer of hospitality.

"I looked at every photo I could find of Li Feng when I got assigned to this detail, so I could get a feel for her. See if I could spot any patterns or vulnerabilities."

"That's good work. I did the same thing."

"Then you see it, too?"

Millie paused to consider.

"She seems a bit off from how the file describes her," Millie said after a moment. "But this is a stressful situation for her, and people don't always act the same under stress."

"Li Feng has been under stress most of her life. This kind of stuff is barely a blip in her day."

Millie nodded along as Mike talked. She was growing more concerned, and frustrated that she hadn't been confident enough in herself to do something about it before a man called it to her attention.

"You're right. I noticed it, too, but wasn't sure it was a big deal."

"I don't believe the woman in that bedroom is Li Feng."

16

BINGO WAS STILL PLANNING HOW TO SPEND HIS BONUS when the security guard from Arrow Donaldson's condo building called to let him know that the Americans had arrived and were on their way up to the penthouse to get Li Feng.

Li Feng.

The woman whose family was as responsible as the Chinese government for what had happened to his wife, and led him to working for a man like Ziggy Peng. After the government had murdered his lead programmer on the deepfake video app team, they sent Bingo's wife to a work camp—and threatened to do the same to Bingo unless he agreed to go undercover to stop the Americans from recruiting high-level spies with gambling addictions. They put him in touch with Arrow Donaldson, who pawned him off on Ziggy Peng to do the dirty business they didn't want to be traced back to themselves.

Bingo thought of his wife, ripped away from their house in the middle of the night. Later he'd found out from Arrow Donaldson that the real reason the government punished him was because he refused to sell his app to QuiTel for peanuts.

He would use his bonus from killing the American woman and attacking Li Feng to hire an investigator who'd had much success finding people who'd run afoul of the government. Those who survived were mostly dumped into the labor camps that were off the grid and so primitively run that Bingo's hacking skills were useless in tracking her.

Bingo pushed those thoughts out of his head so he could concentrate on the task at hand. First he had to hack into the drone. Fate was with him that day, as the drone was assigned to an aerial patrol route very close to the building where Li Feng was staying, making it easier to reroute its path without too much attention. By the time the person monitoring the drone realized something had gone wrong, Bingo would be done.

As the drone approached the penthouse, Bingo typed in the code to raise the window shades in the entire penthouse. Through the monitor showing the feed from the drone's camera, Bingo saw the group of Americans scatter. Then he saw Li Feng.

He forgot about the Americans and he forgot about the bonus. All he could think about was the night that his wife disappeared, and the look on her face as the men with guns dragged her out of the apartment. Li Feng had the same look on her face when Bingo pulled the trigger.

♦ ♦ ♦

Arrow Donaldson had already yanked Millie around once about transferring Li Feng to her custody. She wasn't going to let him get away with doing it a second time. She didn't even care that the woman pretending to be Li Feng could overhear her call.

"Is Li Feng with you yet?" Arrow asked by way of greeting.

"The woman in this apartment is dressed like Li Feng, and she says her name is Li Feng, but I don't—"

"Then your intelligence training should tell you that she *is* Li Feng."

"My intelligence training is telling me that you're lying to me and avoiding transferring Li Feng to my custody once again."

"I knew you were the wrong person for this job. You can't even tell a real person from an impostor."

Determined not to let Arrow get her riled up so she'd say something she'd regret, Millie looked out the window to calm herself—just in time to see a drone buzzing outside. She assumed one of the agents was playing a joke on her and was about to yell at the group when the drone began firing. Millie dove toward the woman posing as Li Feng while one of the agents fired at the drone with an assault rifle.

When the drone finally exploded, Millie waved for the

agent to go and track down as much of the drone's wreckage as he could find. Her attention was focused on the woman bleeding in the middle of the room. Millie wondered if she should call in an emergency response team. But once she was standing over the woman, she realized the woman definitely wasn't Li Feng, and the woman definitely wasn't alive.

17

ZIGGY PENG HUNG UP WITH BINGO AND WONDERED WHAT to do with Dale Gai. He was feeling less guilty about hitting her and angrier that she had made him resort to that kind of primal response. Despite his reputation as a violent man, Ziggy Peng didn't think of himself that way. He didn't get into fights over petty matters, he didn't carry grudges, and he took no particular enjoyment in hurting others. In his line of work, violence was often just the only way to solve a problem. Dale Gai was a problem.

It raised his suspicions that she'd been talking to Stone Barrington, even though Ziggy had been led to believe that Stone Barrington had left the casino with the rest of his loud and obnoxious family and friends. This whole mess—this silly, elaborate plan at the behest of Li

Feng—was layer upon layer of ridiculous deceit. Ziggy left his office and went to a small cubicle in the workroom where he liked to watch security footage. He typed in the keywords needed to bring up the video feed from the time Dale Gai was talking to Stone Barrington in the security suite.

After watching the conversation forward and backward several times, he used the mouse to draw a box around Stone Barrington's face, copied the image, and then pasted it into a box off to the side of the video feed. The casino's facial recognition software would pull up any other video feeds from the last seven days that matched. Nothing came up.

Ziggy rewound the video feed back to the time he knew Stone Barrington checked in and switched to the camera views from the front desk. When he found video of Stone checking in, he did the same search. This time multiple video results came up, but not the conversation with Dale Gai. Ziggy grunted in disgust and went back to the bookmarked video of the conversation with Dale Gai. It was obvious to him now that someone had pretended to be Stone Barrington, and that Dale Gai had seemed to have known.

He zoomed in on their conversation and saw her give a room number to the impersonator before walking away. On his way out of the security suite, Ziggy retrieved a black pole the hotel security used for disengaging the security bars on locked room doors, a contingency used mostly in the event that they suspected a guest may have fallen sick within a locked room. It was time to pay a visit to Dale Gai.

18

TEDDY REMOVED HIS STONE BARRINGTON DISGUISE AND made it to the room Dale Gai had mentioned to him with five minutes to spare. Dale quickly pulled Teddy into the room and slammed the door shut behind him. She looked tired, and the right side of her face was red and swollen.

A tea service sat on the table in the far corner of the room, and Dale went to pour a cup.

"Would you like jasmine tea?" she asked Teddy.

"Do you have anything with more of a kick?"

They were interrupted by the sound of the lock on the door electronically disengaging. Teddy tensed and spun toward the door. He made a motion with his hand for Dale to remain quiet. She took a step back and picked the teapot up off the table. Teddy silently moved toward the door as it opened.

Dale had engaged the security bar, so the door could only open so far. Teddy was preparing to slam the door shut when a thin black pole with a hook on the end poked through the opening and disengaged the security bar.

Teddy waited until he saw a foot inside the doorway, then he pulled the door back before smashing it forward into whoever was on the other side.

He heard the pole drop and threw the door all the way open. Ziggy Peng was in a crumpled heap halfway in the hallway and halfway in the room. Teddy picked up the pole with one hand and with his other he dragged Peng into the room by his shirt.

Peng quickly regained his composure and hopped to his feet. Dale threw the teapot at Peng's head with perfect aim and it exploded in a spray of ceramic and liquid. The commotion gave Teddy enough time to get both hands around the pole and take a swing at Peng's head.

Two handguns and a rifle were locked away securely and unhelpfully in Stone Barrington's suite, and he was defending them from the rogue chief of casino security with a metal pole and pieces of a broken teapot.

Peng was still down, clawing at his burning skin when Teddy smacked him again in the head with the pole. Peng finally went still, and Teddy stepped back in relief. He started to turn to check on Dale, but Peng twitched, then jumped to his feet and reached for the pole in Teddy's hand. Teddy's instincts and training gave him the advantage, and he spun away from Peng and swung the pole backward over his shoulder. When the pole connected with Peng's head, Teddy heard an explosion.

A small hole appeared in the middle of Peng's forehead seconds before he fell backward onto the floor. Teddy turned to see Dale Gai holding an ornate derringer in her hand.

Teddy raised his eyebrows but said nothing . . . for now. Her aim with the gun and the teapot were better than any mere assistant's should have been, but there was no time for clarifications on her skill set.

"Is that a clean gun or registered to you?"

"Clean."

"Do you have any sentimental attachment to it?"

"I was going to wipe it down, then throw it away."

"That's my girl."

"We need to get out of here."

19

MILLIE RODE IN THE BACK OF THE SUV WHILE ONE OF THE other agents drove. They'd thrown the wreckage from the drone into the cargo area of the SUV for the CIA's tech guys to examine at a covert warehouse near the pier. The drive to the warehouse only took about five minutes according to the clock on the dashboard, but to Millie it felt like a decade. By the time they pulled up to the warehouse, Millie's tension and fear had been replaced by disgust and anger. She knew Arrow Donaldson was behind this. His file outlined a long history of intimidation tactics and punitive behavior. She knew he bankrupted innocent businessmen who got in his way, tied up all his opponents in endless legal battles, and engaged in public mudslinging against anybody who tried to fight back.

But she'd never believed he could kill an innocent woman.

As she looked around the area surrounding the warehouse, Millie realized she'd probably made a mistake leaving the penthouse. She tried to convince herself that they'd been in danger, that the woman was only the first target and the rest of the team would have been next, but she knew that wasn't the case. Once the drone was shot down, the danger had been eliminated.

As if on cue to confirm her suspicions that her move had been a bad one, another black SUV, with the look of a U.S. government vehicle, pulled into the lot. Two men in gray suits got out and came over to Millie. They both flashed badges that Millie recognized as CIA, but only one of them talked.

"I'm Agent Parks and this is Agent Malmon. We're with the Agency's Office of Inspector General."

Millie's stomach dropped, but she tried her best to keep the fear off her face as she held out her hand for Agent Parks to shake.

"Millie Martindale. I'm here at the request of Lance Cabot."

"We're aware of your assignment here. We operate independently and report to Director Cabot as well as to the ranking members of the congressional intelligence committees."

"Thank you for the thorough explanation," Millie said. "What can I help you with?"

She held out hope that this was just follow-up on the

casino assignment and would be over with quickly. But that hope was dashed when Agent Parks frowned and stepped back from her.

"We're here about the drone in your vehicle," he said.

Her stomach sank almost to her feet this time. She continued trying to regulate her reactions and her emotions, but she had one big question and she didn't realize until it was too late that she'd asked it out loud.

"How did you get here so quickly?"

"That's an odd question to ask," Agent Parks said.

"I just . . . Normally it seems like it takes forever to get anything done around here. You know?"

She thought that was a competent enough answer. Agent Parks went from looking at her skeptically to looking at her condescendingly. That she could deal with.

"We're going to need to get into your vehicle and to talk to the other members of your team."

"Sure. Of course. Whatever you need."

As Agents Parks and Malmon left her to begin interviewing her colleagues, a white van pulled into the lot and a group of black-clad men and women emerged and began putting on gloves and pulling out bags of gear. An evidence collection team from the CIA. After efficient preparation, the group swarmed Millie's SUV and pushed her agents into the waiting hands of Parks and Malmon. Millie wondered if there was a similar team combing through the penthouse they'd left behind. She marveled again at how this response team had been pulled together so quickly.

As she watched the OIG agents and the evidence team

do their work, Millie was happy that no one seemed interested in her for the time being. She had one contact who couldn't be controlled by anyone. She stepped back further out of view, and called a man most people in the Agency still thought was dead.

"You asked me about Macau earlier," she said when he answered.

"I don't work that way."

"What way is that, might I ask?"

"I like mutually beneficial relationships."

Millie stopped to think. If she involved this man, accepted help from him, there'd be a price to pay, and no turning back.

She didn't like it at all, but Millie Martindale was out of options.

"A woman died."

"Women die every day. Why should I care?"

"This one was pretending to be Li Feng."

"Pretend I don't know who that is."

"Should I also pretend you don't know who Arrow Donaldson is? Should I pretend you don't know who Lance Cabot is?"

"We both know that's ridiculous."

"You called me, remember. And I assume you haven't tried to break into the CIA database yet because I haven't heard anything about it."

"I'd be smarter than that."

Millie sighed, realizing what he meant. "I'm guessing you called a certain basement in Washington, D.C., and found out everything you needed to know."

"I'm very resourceful."

Millie had had just about enough of the patronizing banter and it looked like her time to herself in the parking lot was drawing to a close. The evidence team was loading their gear back into their van, and Agents Parks and Malmon were starting to eye her every so often as they finished talking to her team.

"We're both in Macau and you probably thought it was for separate reasons," Millie said. "But I'd be willing to bet that we're both here for the same reason and that it has something to do with Arrow Donaldson."

There was silence on the other end of the line for a few seconds.

Then: "I'll call you back in a few minutes and we'll tell each other everything we know."

He hung up before Millie could call him a liar.

◆ ◆ ◆

Arrow Donaldson sat in the back of a dark sedan watching the chaos unfold in the parking lot of the warehouse complex, where the GPS tracer in the drone wreckage had led him. It had been a stroke of dumb luck that the CIA's inspector general already had agents in Macau due to suspicions arising from their fishing expedition in his casino with Lance Cabot. But Arrow was not a man to just rely on dumb luck. He knew how to harness good fortune, to amplify it, and to manipulate it. His driver handed him a satellite phone.

"I'm watching it now, Senator. The timing was perfect. Yes. I know about that. The rest will take care of itself. Thank you."

He handed the phone back to his driver. Then he said, "Take me to the bunker."

20

DALE AND TEDDY ESCAPED THE GOLDEN DESERT CASINO through a series of tunnels and passages that hotel security used to get VIPs in and out of the casino without being spotted by fans or anyone else who might make their lives difficult. Once again, Teddy noticed Dale navigated the situation better than any assistant should be expected to. He wondered how many times she'd been in these tunnels herself and under what circumstances.

They exited the casino in the back near the power plant and trash maintenance area. The air was thick with an acrid smell and Teddy choked a bit when he emerged into the air. Small clusters of workers were about, but no one seemed to take notice of them. They walked around toward the front of the casino where Teddy followed

Dale onto a bus. She paid the fare for them both and guided Teddy toward the back.

It clearly wasn't Dale Gai's first time in those clandestine tunnels, and he had to wonder if their use was part of her regular job duties, or if she'd practiced a contingency plan for this kind of escape. In either case, it didn't do anything to calm his misgivings about her. He still didn't fully trust Dale Gai.

They were quiet as the bus made its way down the length of the Cotai Strip toward Coloane Village. Eventually, Dale said, "This was always the end of my plan. Where should we go next?"

Before Teddy could answer, his phone rang, and the screen told him it was Millie Martindale on the other end. They went back and forth about what they knew and how they could help each other. While Teddy was talking, the bus came to a stop and Teddy saw a sign that triggered an idea. He told Millie he would call her back, then he motioned for Dale to follow him off the bus.

Teddy pointed to a sign when they were off the bus to explain his thinking.

"I don't read Chinese as well as I used to, but my Portuguese is still good, and I believe that sign is for the film festival. Right?"

"Very good," Dale said.

"I've been so caught up thinking about this video that I haven't looked more into the shakedown and protection aspect of this thing."

"Okay," Dale said, with a mix of confusion and condescension.

"Peter said his film set was attacked before they got the letter with the video."

Dale nodded, but this time her face lit up as she realized where Teddy was going with all of this.

"You want to go to the film set?"

It was Teddy's turn to nod this time.

"I should have thought of that," Dale said.

"Neither of us is at the top of our game, it seems, but we're still better than everyone else who can help, so let's not get down on ourselves too much."

"They were shooting all over town, but the production offices are just down the road here as a matter of fact," Dale said.

"Can we walk it?"

"Maybe fifteen minutes."

"Okay," Teddy said.

The walk was nice as the area was slightly less crowded and noisy than the main strip. This area was mostly upscale spa resorts without any gambling, as well as other businesses native to residential areas such as grocery stores and home goods stores. The production offices for Peter and Ben's Macau joint venture were in a two-story building detached from a small shopping mall designed more like something from the French Quarter in New Orleans than the more gleaming and modern buildings closer to the casinos.

As they made their way inside, Teddy was pleased to notice a small plaque with the Centurion Studios name and logo on it. It made him feel at home. It also gave him an idea of what to do next and how to investigate without appearing too suspicious. He sat down behind one of the desks in the office, put his feet up, and leaned back casually.

"I'm an employee of Centurion Studios," he said.

"Right. Billy Barnett."

Looking around the office, Teddy's unease with the situation dissipated. Peter and Ben had worked in that office to help make the film industry of Macau better. They could easily have piggybacked onto the more successful Chinese or Hong Kong film markets if they'd wanted to break into the continent, but they'd gone with Macau because Macau needed more help. At their hearts, Peter and Ben were good guys. Teddy would find a way to make sure their good deed didn't end up punishing them.

"Sometimes it's good to stay in the background and watch and wait. But there are other times when I've had great success drawing attention to myself and seeing what I can shake loose."

Teddy took his feet off the desk and looked through the drawers for anything that might help direct his next move. Since Billy Barnett was a Centurion Studios employee, his idea was to tour the areas where Peter and Ben had been filming, with the excuse that he had just arrived from America and was getting caught up on the details. But he wasn't sure where they had been filming or what sets had been attacked. Dale Gai was no help, either.

"I helped them at the resort with their film festival business and security. My responsibilities did not extend outside the casino," Dale said.

There wasn't much left in the office, none of the filming logs that should have been kept, so Teddy was left to improvise. Luckily Teddy was an expert at improvisation.

The only thing of consequence Teddy found in the production office was a dirty business card written in Chinese characters that looked like it had been printed in the back of a moving truck. He handed it over to Dale to read.

Dale looked down at the card, smiled, and handed it back to Teddy.

"I'm not going to like this, am I?" he asked.

"It's for a man named Kwok Lin. He's the head of security for Moonlit Sonata Films."

"That sounds good," Teddy said.

"It would be good if Kwok Lin wasn't so stupid."

21

THE CAMERA ON BINGO'S DRONE WAS DESTROYED WHEN the Americans shot it, but Bingo was able to hack into the municipal camera system and track the Americans as they sped away toward a waterfront warehouse. Once he saw agents pick up pieces of the drone and load them into their vehicles, he knew they would eventually trace them and come up with the programming code he'd used with Sonny Ma's digital fingerprints all over it.

His work was done, so he headed back to the casino to check in with Ziggy Peng. And to see if Dale Gai had managed to get herself into any more trouble.

Nobody paid attention to Dale Gai except Bingo. Well, nobody paid attention to anything other than Dale Gai's looks except Bingo. Bingo was not interested in romantic entanglements, but Dale Gai intrigued him.

She was smarter than the other security assistants who had worked with Ziggy Peng, though Ziggy didn't seem to realize it.

Dale Gai had only been working at the casino for a month the first time Bingo encountered her. At first, he suspected she was a spy. Then he wondered if she was looking for revenge against someone in the organization. Eventually, though, he figured out that she was none of those things. She appeared to be playing a long game, more focused on Arrow Donaldson than any of the people involved in the day-to-day operations of the casino. No one else was smart enough to figure this out, and Bingo wasn't going to let on what he knew, so he continued to watch to see if one day Dale Gai would do something he could benefit from.

One thing he knew they had in common was a love of gambling. Baccarat was the most popular game at the casino and was very popular among his friends and family because they believed in fate, and baccarat was as pure a game of chance as you could get in a casino. But Bingo, and Dale Gai from what he'd seen, preferred blackjack. It was also popular with the casino crowd, and if you knew what you were doing, you could make some decent money once in a while. He sat down at one of the tables when he returned to the casino, but after a couple of bad hands, he left the table and went to the security suite to find Ziggy Peng.

Ziggy was not in his office and Dale Gai didn't seem to be around, either. Bingo knew better than to ask anyone in the tight-lipped security office if they knew where either of them were, so he let himself unassumingly into Ziggy office. Maybe the man had left a clue as to where he might be or what he might be up to.

He noticed immediately that Ziggy's office chair was pulled up close to the security monitors in the far corner of his office. Bingo had a program on his phone that he used to monitor activity on Ziggy's computer, and it didn't take long to figure out Ziggy had been watching Dale Gai and the American they'd called Stone Barrington. The last bit of video Ziggy had watched was of Dale and Stone entering one of the casino's hotel rooms. Bingo wrote down the number and headed to the room.

22

THE HEAD OF SECURITY FOR MOONLIT SONATA FILMS DID not have a desk at the production office. He did business in a karaoke club favored by local gangsters.

Kwok Lin was waiting for them when Teddy and Dale arrived. He acted like the booth was his private reserved office, but the booth's location was terrible and did not speak highly of Kwok Lin. Teddy suspected he was probably related to someone who owned the club. Teddy also suspected he was related to someone at the film company and that most of what Kwok Lin considered as his career was just being related to the right people.

"We're here about Centurion Studios and the movie they were making with your film company," Teddy said.

Kwok Lin looked at Dale the entire time.

"It wasn't a movie. It was pieces of a movie. No whole."

"Why not a whole movie?"

"The crew was no good. We don't do movies here and now we know why."

"What about the triads?" Teddy asked. "Do they harass the film crews in Macau? Blackmail? Protection?"

"There are no film crews in Macau."

"Ever?"

"Macau is for gambling. Golf. Other relaxation. Movies are made in Hong Kong or . . ."

He gestured broadly in the direction of mainland China.

"Then why would Peter and Ben try to make a movie over here?" Teddy asked.

"The film festival," Dale said.

Kwon Lin nodded in agreement.

"Outreach," he said. "Many people come to watch movies in Macau and many young people study how to make movies in Macau. But nobody works making movies in Macau."

"They all leave?" Teddy asked.

Kwok gave a sigh and a nod. Apparently done with the conversation he said, "I would like to sing a song. Karaoke," Kwok said.

"I don't want any part of that," Teddy said as he got up to leave. He handed the man a wad of bills of indeterminate value and left with Dale.

"It sounds like your business partners were trying to do good and someone wants to take advantage of them," Dale said on the bus back to the office.

"You believed him?"

"Everything he said is true. Filmmakers keep trying to make an industry happen here."

"I guess that's good if the triads aren't involved. Organized crime is never ideal to mess with."

"Kwok Lin is barely a criminal and he is certainly not organized."

"Do you know anything about anyone else in this film company?"

"I fear I have let you down by leading you to believe I know all in Macau," Dale said.

"I have that problem as well," Teddy said.

"People expect movie producers to know much about everything in America?"

"About as much as they expect security assistants at casinos to know."

They were back at the film office. Teddy said he was going to work from the office for a while and invited Dale to stay and work with him.

"I have many responsibilities but thank you. I need to get back to the casino."

"Won't they be looking for you when they find the body in your room?"

"I will be fine. I am not Kwok Lin. I am not stupid."

23

BINGO HAD JUST LET HIMSELF INTO ROOM 5310 WHEN HIS cell phone rang. It was Arrow Donaldson and he briefly thought about ignoring the call, but Bingo made his way through the rest of the room and found the dead body of Ziggy Peng.

"Ziggy Peng is dead."

"What? How?" Arrow asked.

"This was the work of Dale Gai and an American."

"American?"

"He was in disguise, but he's a movie producer named Billy Barnett."

"Why would Dale Gai and an American kill Ziggy Peng?"

"This Billy Barnett seems to be more than a movie

producer. And I think we both realize Dale Gai is more than an assistant."

"Right," Arrow said, slowly. Bingo knew Arrow to be a misogynist. He minimized the women around him at every opportunity, not realizing that it put him at a disadvantage.

"I'm also guessing he knows the attack on the CIA wasn't the work of Sonny Ma."

"We'll deal with that later. I have to figure out what to do about this dead woman. I wonder if we should have just scared them with a minor attack instead of killing her."

"Dead women don't tell their secrets," Bingo said.

♦ ♦ ♦

Arrow disconnected from his call with Bingo and noticed Li Feng staring at him.

"You ask me to trust you, yet you lie at every opportunity?"

"And you lie to me," Arrow yelled, waving his fists at Li Feng and clenching his jaw until his face began to twitch.

"This is *all* built on lies. So many lies."

"I had a plan," Arrow said.

"You had an idea. I helped you make it into a plan."

"You agreed to that plan and for doing me a simple favor, I am going to provide you with a new identity so you can escape the life you have here and pursue whatever nonsense it is you want for your future. This vendetta against Sonny Ma has brought trouble to my organization that threatens to take us all down."

"Your man said something to me in the car that might be relevant now," Li Feng said.

"Do tell."

"He asked me why I didn't just kill Sonny Ma."

"We've all asked that."

"It's not what I wanted at the beginning, but now that there is already a dead woman . . ."

"I'll have Bingo kill this Billy Barnett and pin it all on Sonny Ma," Arrow said.

"That sounds like a plan."

♦ ♦ ♦

Bingo was going to get something to eat when his phone rang. He almost didn't answer it because he thought Arrow Donaldson was calling a third time. But the phone kept buzzing, to the point of distraction, so he took it out and noticed it was Kwok Lin, a local gossip who occasionally had useful information. It didn't take long for Bingo to realize Kwok was calling to tell him about Billy Barnett.

"I've met many Americans and many movie producers. This man was too subtle, too smart, too quiet. It was quite disturbing," Kwok said.

"My patience with this conversation is reaching its end," Bingo said.

"The man was with a woman who works at the Golden Desert Casino. That's Arrow Donaldson's casino."

It should not have surprised him that Dale Gai was involved. Bingo contemplated hanging up on Kwok Lin and going to follow Dale Gai to see what she was up to, but he wondered if he could use this fool first.

"Call the producer back," Bingo said. "Tell him you found out that Sonny Ma is looking to get back into the crime business and this has all the marks of his operation."

"Really? Sonny Ma is looking to get back in the game? I thought he made a bunch of money in the tech field."

"Do as I say. Do not worry about context or truth."

24

TEDDY HUNG UP AFTER TALKING TO KWOK LIN AND frowned. After telling Teddy that the triads had no interest in the nonexistent film industry in Macau, Kwok Lin had called back and told him the opposite.

"You know of famous gangster Sonny Ma? I have some highly placed sources in the underworld, and they say that Sonny Ma is looking to get back to his criminal ways."

From everything Teddy had read about Sonny Ma, this seemed unlikely. From all accounts he'd worked hard after being released from a harsh Chinese prison, and was now making a lot of money in the tech field. He was about to make his biggest investment yet in online gambling, which stood to make him an even wealthier man.

Even a hint of scandal would be enough to blow the whole deal dead.

Maybe Sonny Ma was just a rotten apple who had no choice but to succumb to his criminal temptations, even when the risk was so high. Or, Teddy thought, someone was trying to frame Sonny Ma.

Teddy decided the best thing to do was stick to his original plan of playing the part of the annoying American movie producer, going around to the sites where Peter and Ben had been filming to see if he could shake anything loose. Peter and Ben said they'd been filming at the casino, and Teddy assumed they'd meant the Golden Desert. But according to Dale Gai, they'd been referring to a pawnshop the locals called "the casino one."

♦ ♦ ♦

The pawnshop near the casino was not what Teddy expected. Pawnshops in Macau were used mostly as underground banks to help tourists take out gambling money that the Chinese government wouldn't know about. This pawnshop looked less seedy, more like a warehouse for an upscale auction house.

Even though the location was in the heart of an area that looked like a movie set designer's idea of a Chinese pawnshop neighborhood, the interior of the wide-open space was bright and clean and packed with a highly organized stock of luxury goods. Teddy's entrance was quickly noticed, and a short, elegant older man approached him.

"I am the owner here. How can I help you?" the man said.

"I'm a producer for Centurion Studios and wanted to follow up on a lead about filming at this location. I understand my colleagues already reached out to you?"

"Oh. The movie."

The old man looked as if Teddy had just told him that his entire family had died. He stumbled backward a few steps, then took a seat behind the main counter of the store.

"Are you okay?" Teddy asked.

"I'm just tired of all of this. All dreams and no reality."

"A strange perspective coming from a man who makes his living from the casinos."

"I do not make my living from the casinos. I provide a mutually beneficial service, yes, but the casinos could go away tomorrow and I would still have my business."

"My colleagues, two Americans. Did you talk to them?"

Teddy watched the old man's face before he answered. The man wasn't trying to place Peter or Ben, he was constructing a lie. Teddy had seen enough of it in his years with the CIA, and he'd trained plenty of agents himself on how to do it better. This man likely had to lie quite a bit professionally, but he looked uncomfortable lying to Teddy.

"They wanted to use my business to make their movie."

"Did you agree to that?"

"No. There were rumors that things had happened at their other locations. I didn't want to put my people in danger."

"There were attacks at other locations?"

The man nodded and crossed his right hand over his left in front of him on the counter.

"What did you hear about the attacks?" Teddy asked.

The man leaned closer to Teddy like he was about to tell him a secret, then he smiled crookedly and leaned back in his chair.

"No. I'm not a gossip. I'm no fan of criminals, but once a man has paid his debt to society, I have no business with how he spends his time."

Teddy felt like he was playing an amateur-hour game show, but the old man seemed to be enjoying himself.

"You would have been paid for letting them use your business, right?" Teddy asked.

"As I told you—I always find a way to make a living, with or without the casinos."

"It seems a shame that rumors of an attack would cost you a good deal."

"It is heartbreaking," the man said. "The total would have been substantial."

Teddy reached into his pocket and pulled out a stack of bills and handed them to the man.

"I'm sorry to hear about these events. Centurion hopes to be a good ambassador of the American film industry, not to cause trouble."

"Thank you."

"I don't carry substantial amounts of cash on me, but I do hope that can help with the goodwill we would have enjoyed while working together highlighting your beautiful city."

"You are a good man, Mr. . . ."

"Barnett. Billy Barnett," Teddy said, holding out his hand across the counter. "Centurion Studios."

"You are a good man, Mr. Billy Barnett," the man said, shaking Teddy's hand, "unlike Sonny Ma."

Teddy didn't like where this was going. The story was too easy. It fit too perfectly with Kwok Lin's revised story. Teddy never trusted anything that was too easy.

"Sonny Ma attacked the other film sets?" Teddy asked.

"Not himself, of course. He is above that now from his high-tech penthouse apartment. But he still commands respect on the street. It would be easy for him to find many men to do this in his name."

"Is it possible that Sonny Ma doesn't know these things are being done in his name?"

That possibility was immediately diffused by the horrified look on the old man's face.

"*Nothing* is done in Sonny Ma's name without Sonny Ma's permission."

"Maybe he's too busy with his new investment to keep up with what's happening on the street the way he used to," Teddy said.

"The street is his life. It's his identity. They are showing a movie about him at the film festival, all about his criminal life."

"I'd heard that."

"Sonny Ma authorized the film," the old man said. "Sonny Ma will be at the premiere. Sonny Ma bathes in this image."

"That seems dangerous to his new investment opportunity."

"It's his brand. He needs a way to stand out, and his criminal background makes his gambling product more enticing."

Teddy wasn't sure he bought that, but he'd gotten enough from the old man to help with the rest of his investigation. They shook hands again and Teddy headed back to the casino to see if he could find Dale.

◆ ◆ ◆

When Billy Barnett left the pawnshop, Bingo emerged from the back office where he'd been watching the visit on the security monitors.

"You told him what he needed to hear?" Bingo asked the old man.

"I gave him as much truth as I could spare to make him believe."

Bingo wondered if the man was lying. The audio on the security feed was terrible and Bingo had missed much of what was said.

"You're not lying to me?"

"No, sir."

The man looked at the ground at Bingo's feet. Even though he'd done terrible things and would do many more, Bingo hated being an intimidating presence. It made him uncomfortable. Intimidation was for people like Ziggy Peng who were evil, lacking in empathy. Bingo told the old man to look at him. The eye contact was awkward, but Bingo kept it until the look of terror was gone from the old man's face.

"You've been very helpful. Thank you. You have my gratitude, and you have Arrow Donaldson's gratitude."

25

TEDDY WAS HALFWAY BACK TO THE CASINO WHEN HE sensed someone following him. He wasn't sure how long he'd had the tail, but he'd likely picked it up shortly after leaving the pawnshop. His gut instinct had told him the story he'd been fed by the old man was nonsense—now he knew he'd been spot-on.

Glancing in a storefront window, he spotted the tail that was a block back. The man didn't seem to be trying too hard to avoid being seen—either he was an amateur, or he wanted Teddy to know he was there. Teddy slowed his walk, and the tail seemed to speed up. He looked to be getting himself in position to make a move. Teddy didn't think the man wanted to kill him—not in such a public place—which was a relief because, once again, Teddy found himself without a weapon. Nevertheless,

Teddy was on high alert, hoping to turn this into an opportunity. Maybe the tail had information worth knowing about what was really going on.

When the man was just a few feet back, Teddy moved toward a small group of European tourists. Teddy was a legend of disguise, but that didn't mean he was only good with wigs and makeup. After studying with the world's greatest actors, mimes, illusionists, and hunters, Teddy was able to see how they contorted their bodies and faces into new shapes and used natural cover to manipulate what was right in front of someone. This knowledge and years of practice in high-stress operations gave Teddy the skills and comfort level to make himself virtually invisible in a public space.

By the time his tail realized Teddy was behind him, Teddy had maneuvered the man off into an alley and quietly disarmed and subdued him.

"We haven't met yet," Teddy said, "but I feel like we already know so much about one another."

The man squirmed quietly but was unable to get out from under Teddy's grasp.

"This city brings out the dealmaker in me. So, instead of killing you right here and dumping you in one of the many convenient trash bins along this street, I'm going to give you a choice."

The man continued to squirm, getting harder to control. His grunts and growls were also getting louder through Teddy's hands.

"I need information and I need it quicker than going from person to person looking for the right piece of the puzzle at the right time. We're going to go to the casino and play baccarat while you give me the answers I need. No one dies and maybe we even walk away with a few more bucks in our pockets."

The man didn't answer in any discernible way, but he continued to struggle. It was getting to the point where Teddy would have had trouble controlling him discreetly. Finally, tired of the whole thing, Teddy slipped one of several small syringes he kept in his coat pocket into his hand and jabbed the man in the leg.

♦ ♦ ♦

In the taxi back to the casino, Teddy pretended he was trying to keep his drunk friend awake while searching his tail's pockets. He found the man's wallet and learned the man's name was Bing-Wen Jo. Based on what Kevin had told him about Bingo doing Arrow's dirty work around Macau, Teddy had suspected the man's identity. But confirmation was always nice. The mild tranquilizer was wearing off and Teddy had Bingo's arm over his shoulder, stumbling them across the floor as if he were bringing his drunken friend back to their room.

When the tranquilizer had fully worn off, Teddy and Bingo stood at an empty baccarat table with drinks in hand. Bingo had a glassy look in his eyes as he took several slow sips from his drink.

"Let's get started," Teddy said.

Bingo nodded.

Teddy wondered if he'd measured the medication

properly, because Bingo should have been fully recovered from the dose he'd been given. Had he used the wrong syringe?

"I always wanted to be James Bond," Teddy said to the dealer, "but it's harder than it looks."

26

WHEN AGENTS MALMON AND PARKS FINALLY MADE THEIR way over to interview Millie, she was ready.

"We talked to the agents at the hotel before we came over here," Parks said.

"Good," Millie said.

"They weren't exactly complimentary of you or your leadership skills."

"Leaders sometimes have to tell people who work for them that they're morons. Those people don't generally appreciate the criticism and therefore speak poorly of their leaders."

"Their concern was less with your tone or what you called them and more with your . . . lack of leadership skills."

"You mean my lack of . . . Can I say 'balls' to you?

Will that offend you? Will it show poor leadership on my part?"

"Very funny, Ms. Martindale, but it does seem their concerns about how you handled this operation were justified."

"I was supposed to discern not only that the woman in that penthouse was a decoy, but to anticipate that she would be gunned down by a hijacked drone?"

"How did you know the drone was hijacked?" Parks asked, trying to raise an eyebrow suspiciously, but only succeeding in looking like he was twitching.

"Of course it was hijacked. Unless you believe the Chinese military was trying to kill a woman pretending to be a spy."

As Millie said the words, it dawned on her that maybe the drone *hadn't* been hijacked. Maybe the Chinese government really did aim to kill the woman for some reason.

"Do you have reason to believe the Chinese government *wasn't* behind this?" Parks asked.

"I can't divulge the details of my operation, but I can tell you that the Chinese government would have known that woman wasn't Li Feng."

Millie had thought she was ready for this conversation. She'd planned to give short, respectful answers that provided enough information that she'd appear compliant without taking any blame for what happened. She hadn't absolved herself of the guilt, but she would talk to Lance and deal with it appropriately. She would not let some internal affairs jerks likely sent by Arrow Donaldson get to her.

It wasn't going great, but she was hoping she could still turn the conversation her way until she heard the helicopter overhead.

Everyone in the parking lot looked up and watched it land. Millie expected Arrow Donaldson to step out, which made it even more surprising when she saw her boyfriend, FBI agent Quentin Phillips, emerge from the helicopter and walk toward her.

"Who are you?" Agent Parks asked.

Quentin brushed passed him and stood shoulder-to-shoulder with Millie.

"Quentin Phillips. I'm with the FBI."

"Ms. Martindale is a CIA officer and therefore under the jurisdiction of—"

"I have a letter here signed by the president of the United States that demands you stand down and let Ms. Martindale get back to work."

"The FBI has no jurisdiction in China."

"I'd think the seal and signature of the president would be enough to calm your territorial instincts, but since that doesn't seem to be the case, I'll let you in on a little secret. The drone that was shot down was hacked through a network of servers, one of which is in the United States of America. The drone itself was built with schematics that are alleged to have been stolen from a United States defense company. That's corporate espionage, and that's FBI jurisdiction."

Parks and Malmon looked at each other with confused irritation before stepping away to confer with each other. When they returned, Agent Malmon spoke for the first time.

"This isn't over."

"Have your boss call my boss and we'll set up a playdate," Quentin said.

Malmon and Parks argued all the way back to their car while Quentin put his arm around Millie in an awkward side hug. She pushed him back with a wry smile.

"I can fight my own battles, you know," Millie said. "I don't need a man to rescue me."

"The president, who authorized my visit to rescue you, is a woman," Quentin said.

27

"I FEEL LIKE WE SHOULD BE IN TUXEDOS FOR THIS TO work," Teddy said, again to the dealer, because he was the only one responsive at the table. Bingo was still staring vacantly off into the distance and ignoring Teddy's conversation. Teddy had briefly wondered if Bingo was only acting zoned out so that he didn't have to answer Teddy's questions, but after a few quick tests to see if he could catch Bingo off guard, Teddy concluded the vacant stare was real.

He was about ready to give up and take Bingo back to Stone's suite—to use more traditional means of information extraction—when a waitress walked by and asked if he'd like a drink.

"Lemon tea for my friend," Teddy said.

The woman smiled and nodded, returning several

minutes later with an elegant ceramic teacup steaming with a thick yellow-tinted liquid. Teddy tipped her and the dealer well, then played a few hands to reacquaint himself with the game while the calming properties of the lemon and hot tea hopefully cleared the remainder of the tranquilizer from Bingo's system. A few hands in, Teddy noticed the life coming back to Bingo's eyes.

"Deal my friend in this time," Teddy said.

Teddy knew the odds in baccarat, like everything else, were in the house's favor, but the margin was as slim as possible and had great potential for careful players to win considerable amounts. This is how Teddy saw his interaction with Bingo. He could have played the easy odds and killed him, but the payoff would have been minimal. Playing this game, buying time with Bingo, had the potential to net very useful information if Teddy was patient.

"Tie," the dealer said, pulling Teddy's attention back to the table.

Teddy had his wager on the player's hand and Bingo's was on the banker's hand. Two rounds in a row there'd been a tie. This time Teddy moved both wagers to the player's hand, where the payoff was better.

"If you win, you keep the cash and tell me who sent you," Teddy said.

Bingo nodded, though Teddy wasn't completely sure he was coherent. Even so, it wasn't so much specific information he was hoping to get from Bingo. Playing the game would give them time together, which would up the chances that the drugs in Bingo's system would cause him to spill something he normally wouldn't.

They were playing at the mini-baccarat table, so there was less ceremony and the game went quicker because there was less money at stake. The dealer dealt the player's hand first with a total of seven, and Teddy waved off another card.

"That's very good for us," Teddy said.

The dealer then dealt his own hand which totaled nine, beating the player's hand.

"Looks like I don't have to tell you anything," Bingo said.

Two more hands, two more shifts in wagers, and Teddy managed to lose both. After twenty minutes of poor game play, Teddy's patience was running thin and more players were joining the table, making conversation difficult.

"Tell me what's going on with the film set attacks and the blackmail letter to my partners," Teddy said.

"Seven hands in a row your hand has either tied or lost. I don't have to tell you anything."

"I can't say this is how I imagined things going, but I think we both remember the look on your face in that alley when I was on top of you and could have easily snapped your neck."

"It seems to me," Bingo said, finishing off the last of his tea, "that you can't even manage to drug me properly, let alone kill me."

"One more hand. Last chance."

"This game is ridiculous. I'm leaving."

Teddy let Bingo walk away and get far enough away that he had to hurry up to reach him when he left the table. It gave the illusion of a drunk friend catching up to his buddy while providing cover for Teddy to stumble into Bingo and jab him with another syringe. Teddy had his arm around Bingo and kept a firm grip on him even as Bingo wriggled to escape.

"This one was poison," Teddy said. "Maybe I put too much in this one, too. Who knows?"

"You're bluffing."

"Maybe. That will be up to you to decide. I've got the antidote back in my hotel room, and it's all yours when my questions are answered satisfactorily."

"Let me go."

Teddy released Bingo from his grip.

"I trust you know where to find me if you change your mind," Teddy said.

"You aren't the first person to poison me and you won't be the last."

28

BINGO WENT TO THE OWNER'S SUITE AT THE GOLDEN DES-ert, hoping Arrow Donaldson would be there. When it was clear Arrow was away, Bingo let himself in and called his boss.

"I know this number," Arrow said, "and I don't remember giving anyone permission to use that room."

"It seems to me that if you can't trust a man in your hotel room, you shouldn't be trusting him with anything important in your life."

"Why are you calling?"

"I just got back from playing baccarat with Billy Barnett."

"I never did get that game. I know it's big over here, and I still seem to make money from it, but it makes no sense to me."

"I can't figure out what his play was with it. I think he was trying to get inside my head, but he also seemed to be joking around."

"Seems like what I would expect from those Hollywood weirdos. Did you kill him?"

"It wasn't that kind of situation. He seemed like he was genuinely looking for information about his colleagues. I don't think he has any idea what's going on here. I should have just told him Sonny Ma was behind everything and been done with it."

"That sure does sound like what I'm paying you to do."

"I wanted to see what game he was trying to play with me."

"I thought you said you were playing baccarat," Arrow said.

Bingo often wondered at men like Arrow, who rose to such positions of power with seemingly so little intellect. "I meant at the wider level. Billy Barnett is a man who seems like he plays the long game."

"Then Billy Barnett sounds like a man who needs to die."

"No. His death would bring too many questions. But I think I can make him believe what we want him to believe."

"I don't get it. You make him sound like some kind of genius James Bond in one breath, and then you turn around and make him sound gullible. Which is it?"

"Billy Barnett is a complicated man who is more valuable to us alive than dead."

♦ ♦ ♦

Bingo waited until the middle of the night before going to the room where Billy Barnett was staying and banging on the door as loudly as he could. At that time of night he expected Barnett to be tired and disheveled, but when he opened the door, he seemed alert and well-rested. He'd been expecting Bingo.

"I know you didn't really poison me," Bingo said.

Billy Barnett nodded and waved Bingo into the hotel room.

"Come in. I'll pour you a drink."

Bingo took a long swallow of the amber liquid Billy Barnett offered him and felt his plan coming together better in his head.

"That's Knob Creek," Billy Barnett continued. "A friend of mine swears by it. I drink when I need to, socially it's frowned upon to be any kind of teetotaler, but I prefer water most of the time."

Once again, Bingo had no idea what kind of game Barnett was playing with him. It was fascinating as much as it was frustrating. Bingo finished the rest of the drink and took a bottle of water next when Barnett offered. He decided whatever game it was needed a wild card, and the best wild card Bingo knew of was the truth.

"What's your game here?" Bingo asked.

"It's not baccarat. That was excruciating."

"Seriously. What do you want with me?"

"I should ask you the same thing. First you follow me, then you won't tell me anything about who sent you. I had to resort to threats, but you came anyway even though you knew I didn't poison you. Why?"

"You're different from everyone else who comes through town, and that intrigues me. I've grown . . . disillusioned with my current job situation and I'm on the lookout for new potential partners."

"It seems like whatever plan you're a part of is being improvised as we all go along, and I think you're smart enough to realize that means things may not turn out well for you. Whoever's holding your leash isn't as good as he thinks he is."

To that, Bingo made no reply.

Teddy gave him a level look. "Which means, we may be able to help each other."

As Bingo watched this movie producer command the room so completely, and diagnose Bingo's strategy and interest so quickly, it was the first time he felt optimistic that he might be able to leave Arrow Donaldson. It was becoming clear to Bingo that even though he projected an image of business savvy and danger, Arrow Donaldson was nothing more than a lucky and stupid man ready to fall.

Bingo had started pushing back against Arrow—his dramatic and overcomplicated plans—and to Bingo's surprise, the man put up with a shocking level of insubordination. It seemed as if Arrow knew he was on a slow downward spiral, and was desperately clinging to anyone who could help him. But eventually, this plan with Li Feng would bring him down, and Bingo didn't want to be dragged along with him. This Billy Barnett, or whoever he really was, seemed a better bet for Bingo.

"How do you know you can trust me?" Bingo asked.

"I don't," Teddy said, almost cheerfully. "I don't trust anyone. Tell me about Sonny Ma."

"Sonny Ma is a brand more than a person. An urban legend."

"They're showing a movie about him at the film festival, I hear," Teddy said.

"Nonsense propaganda at best."

"His name keeps coming up, but he doesn't seem like a man who would benefit from petty street crime like this."

"Sonny Ma loves Macau. He loves his version of Macau, which is stuck in time and doesn't include American casino owners or movie producers. American film companies have been trying to make a movie about his life for years, but Sonny Ma only cooperated with filmmakers from Macau. He sees himself as some kind of hero protector, I think."

"Like Robin Hood?"

"Except Sonny Ma likes to keep more of the money he steals."

"This online gambling thing. It's something he's doing to get back at Arrow Donaldson?"

Bingo nodded. "Teamed up with Arrow's biggest competitor."

Teddy still didn't trust Bingo or know what angle he was playing, but the information he was giving Teddy made more sense than anything else he'd heard since he'd been in Macau. He wasn't sure if that was good or bad, but it was certainly refreshing.

29

BINGO WENT BACK TO HIS HOUSE AND FINALLY ATE, THEN took a nap to sleep off whatever was left of the cocktails Billy Barnett had stabbed him with.

The nap didn't last long. Just as Bingo was entering deep sleep, someone started banging on his door so hard the whole building seemed to shake. Bingo only knew of one person big and stubborn enough to knock like that, and it was not someone Bingo wanted in his house.

Bingo opened the door and found a man he knew only as Gong. It was a name Bingo found offensive, but also appropriate because it referenced how many times the man had been hit in his life. Bingo had hired Gong to attack the Americans' film set. Now that the work was over, Bingo had hoped he'd seen the last of the man.

"What can I help you with, Gong?"

"I need more work."

"I told you when you signed on that this was a temporary job."

"I need to do it again." Bingo could understand why. Arrow Donaldson paid top dollar. It was hard to let go of a good thing.

"There is no more work. Everyone is gone from the set. There's no one to attack."

"That's not what I saw the other day," Gong said.

Bingo paused. "At the production office? Tell me what you saw."

Gong nodded.

"There was a man and a woman working there. The woman had been there before, with the two Americans. This guy was new. American, but older than the others."

"There are several businesses in that building. It doesn't mean that they were doing anything with the movie."

"They weren't just at the office. They went back to the pawnshop where the other two Americans did their filming. The one you wouldn't let me go to."

"Arrow Donaldson said not to attack the pawnshop. It's important to his business."

"I don't care about that. I just want to know if there's going to be more work now that people are back at the movie office."

Gong seemed genuinely excited to get back to work harassing the film sets. Bingo wasn't sure if it was because he hated the American movie people as much as Sonny Ma did, or if he just liked beating people up, and all the better to be paid for it. Either way, Bingo hated to have to tell the imposing man there was no more work on that front.

"That's just a money guy coming in to close things down," Bingo said. "The two men you saw earlier have already gone back to the U.S. I am sorry."

"I can swing a bat at a moneyman, too."

"There will be more work in the future. Don't worry. You did a good job, and that will be remembered."

Gong pushed his way into the house, closed the door behind him, and moved closer toward Bingo.

"I don't need to be remembered. I need to be paid."

Bingo nodded and put his hand on Gong's enormous chest, showing that he wasn't afraid of the man's size or threats. He wasn't afraid, but he also didn't want to make an enemy of the giant man if he didn't have to. He thought back to why he'd originally brought in Gong, who was not a part of his regular crew.

"Sonny Ma really hates the American movie people, doesn't he?" Bingo asked, echoing what he'd told Billy Barnett.

"It's not just Sonny Ma. A lot of us in the streets hate those monsters and what they've done to our city."

"More than what the casinos have done to the city?"

"They are one and the same to me."

"You're part of Sonny Ma's crew, right? Does he even have a crew anymore?"

"It's not an organization. But there are those of us on the street still loyal to him."

"And people know you and Sonny Ma are connected to each other?"

"Yes."

"Come to think of it, I might need you to take one more ride."

If an associate of Sonny Ma's killed Billy Barnett, it would bolster the claim that he was behind the recent crime spree. It would do enough damage to his reputation that Sonny Ma would never be able to show his face in Macau again.

"Do you have any problem killing a man?" Bingo asked.

"I have a harder time *not* killing them."

30

TEDDY WOKE UP THE NEXT MORNING IN STONE BAR-rington's suite at the Grand Desert and decided to act more like Stone without the disguise. He brewed a cup of coffee from the above-average machine in the suite to hold him over until the room service tray arrived with even better coffee, scrambled eggs, fruit, assorted breakfast meats, and a truly decadent French toast and Belgian waffle blend. He ate it all, saving the waffle for the end, then took his English-language newspaper out on the balcony with another cup of coffee.

The newspaper was mostly bland and geared toward those in Macau on business rather than pleasure. Teddy wasn't in town for either, so he sipped his coffee and watched the city come to life below him. When he found himself contemplating a life of travel and luxury with little responsibility, he called Dale Gai and told her to meet him at the production office.

Dale was already there when Teddy arrived, and he was surprised to find himself irritated that she always seemed to be one step ahead of him. Teddy never considered himself particularly petty, but these days he rarely found himself in the presence of anyone whose skills approached his.

Teddy had been spending too much time in L.A., where everyone analyzed everything to death. It seemed like that was creeping into his own mind as well.

"You look refreshed, like a tourist," Dale said when she saw Teddy.

"It's the hotel coffee and waffles."

"It looks good on you."

"It wouldn't if I ate like this every day. I'd be so large you'd have to roll me around town."

"I heard you had quite the adventure the other night with our friend Bing-Wen Jo."

"Were you spying on me?"

"I work in security for one of the biggest casinos in Macau. I'd be angry if I didn't hear about the American movie producer drunkenly playing baccarat with one of the town's most notorious criminals."

"You better never let Arrow Donaldson hear you refer to his casino as *one* of the biggest in the city."

"If I'm lucky, Arrow Donaldson won't hear me refer to anything. Ever. Tell me what you two talked about during your card game."

"We didn't talk much. He just zoned out and didn't give me anything useful."

"You ordered lemon tea for him," Dale said.

"Just because it's a casino doesn't mean people need to drink alcohol all of the time."

Teddy didn't bother asking how or why she knew what he had ordered for Bingo. It was obvious that Teddy had piqued her interest; even when he wasn't around her, she was paying attention to what he was doing. He'd need to remember that.

"You're right. It's probably just a coincidence that lemon tea also happens to be one of the best natural antidotes to tranquilizers."

"I'll pretend not to find it odd that you know that as long as you pretend not to be interested in how *I* know that."

"I'm more interested in why someone would be using tranquilizers to get information from a dangerous criminal in the first place."

"Believe it or not, there are people who don't see violence as the answer to every problem," Teddy said.

"Regardless of the tools or the reasoning, what were the results?"

"As I said, nothing during the card game. But he came back to my room in the middle of the night."

"He had himself a change of heart?"

"I don't think so. I think he's being directed by someone higher up behind the scenes, and for some reason he decided telling me the truth provided him a strategic advantage. He told me a very interesting story about Sonny Ma."

Teddy gave her the full report of what Bingo had told him. She nodded approvingly as he spoke.

"That does make sense," she said.

Teddy unlocked the office and led Dale inside. She took a seat in front of the desk, but before Teddy could join her, he heard motorcycles approaching and looked out the window. By the time he noticed that two motorcycles were headed straight for the window, he was already prepping for an attack. His first instinct was to get Dale out of harm's way, but she was already out of her seat and headed for the door. Teddy looked around, yet again, for a weapon and noticed Dale wasn't having the same issue. She pulled an attack baton from a pocket in her jumpsuit and ran toward the motorcycles.

Each motorcycle had two riders. The driver of the one closest to Dale was the largest man Teddy had ever seen. Dale snapped the baton out to its full length, then expertly launched it into the spokes of the motorcycle next to her.

The bike came to an abrupt and violent stop, tossing off the passenger in the back. The big driver showed surprising grace and agility, tucking himself into a landing and rolling back onto his feet in a few compact moves.

Teddy was out of the office by then, wielding a metal curtain rod inspired by Dale's baton. He took on the giant man while Dale took on the other riders. The other motorcycle was circling back toward Dale, and as the bike came at her, she stepped to the side just enough to avoid being hit and grabbed on to the rider in the back. She used his body to pull herself onto the motorcycle, while pushing him off like an old-time movie cowboy.

Dale reached around the waist of the remaining rider, grabbed the handlebars over his hands, and squeezed the brakes, aiming the motorcycle directly at the other two riders. The collision knocked them all to the ground, but Dale was prepared for the impact. With an agile twist she launched herself away from the bike and tucked her body into a roll, popped back up, and dusted herself off to go help Teddy with the giant.

The big man was strong and stubborn and could take a hit well. Teddy knew how to box, but those moves weren't working against a man who didn't seem to feel pain. Teddy wondered if he was high on drugs or adrenaline. He tried a variety of martial arts moves that had more of an effect, but not enough to bring the big man down.

Out of violent options, Teddy found his greatest success with a series of ballroom dance moves. Along with the lethal training the CIA provided, they also provided social training to help their operatives blend into any situation. On one mission, Teddy had been sent into an east African country run by an enormous female warlord who loved to dance. One of the Agency's instructors had taught Teddy how to lead a dance partner twice his size and still look graceful. The skills translated almost exactly to maneuvering this giant man into enough walls and sharp objects to keep him from beating Teddy to death. He was giving Teddy everything he could handle when Dale joined them.

While Teddy continued attacking from the front, Dale snuck in a few nasty shots to the big man's kidneys and gonads from behind. She finished by jumping on the man's shoulders like an aggressive toddler, swinging her belt around his neck, and pulling it tight. When the giant finally fell to the ground unconscious, Teddy checked to make sure the giant was still breathing. Then he looked to see who else was left. All the other punks had run away scared, but not before lighting the office on fire.

Teddy and Dale rushed into the building to try and put out the flames, but the massive stacks of papers in the office and the age of the building itself caused the conflagration to spread. They quickly made the decision together that they didn't want to be around to answer questions about what they'd been up to when the fire services and police arrived. So after yelling as much as they could for everyone to get out, they walked away.

31

AS THEY WALKED BACK TO THE CASINO FROM THE PRODUC-tion office, Dale was quiet and contemplative. Not one to pry into anyone else's feelings, thus minimizing the risk he'd be asked about his own, Teddy kept quiet, though he assumed the same thing was bothering them both. There was more than just a protection racket going on.

He recognized the motorcycle attack as the work of amateurs rather than a triad. And someone with Dale's skills, and likely experience, would have to be blind not to have come to the same conclusion. Mixed with what he had heard from Millie about Li Feng, and the fact that Bingo's midnight trip to his hotel room for the "anti-dote" seemed staged, Teddy suspected it was all related. Knowing that there were extra layers to whatever trouble was brewing in Macau, Teddy thought the time had come for him to find out who Dale Gai really was.

"You're obviously more than a secretary," Teddy said after several blocks.

"I never said I wasn't."

"You haven't really said anything."

"No more and no less than you."

"Point taken," Teddy said. "But I know who I am, and I know what side I'm on."

"Do you? A man like you, a man who is more than a movie producer, likely only cares about one side: his own."

"My side right here and right now is the side of Peter Barrington and Ben Bacchetti and Centurion Studios. They're good men doing good work and they're being punished for it. That doesn't sit right with me."

"It doesn't sit right with me, either. That's why I've been helping."

Teddy slowed his walk and looked her over. She seemed genuine. But, of all people, Teddy knew how much appearances could deceive.

"There are so many unknowns and so many moving pieces in this game that I find myself looking for the simplest answers, the easiest explanations," Teddy said. "And the simplest explanation is that you're a spy for Arrow Donaldson and you've been assigned to keep an eye on me and make sure I don't get in the way of what's really going on."

"You disappoint me, Billy Barnett."

"I don't live my life defined by disappointments, my own or anyone else's."

"You know life isn't simple. Answers aren't simple. *You* aren't simple."

"You don't know me."

"I know you as much as you think you know me," Dale said. "Everything you think I am, I *used* to be. I was a spy and a killer, and I was good at it. But I got out. I wanted to travel without having a target to kill, and I wanted to spend some of the money I earned."

"Then why are you here, working at the casino?"

"I like to gamble. It's fun. And I like the Golden Desert. It's my home. And my home is rotten."

"Arrow Donaldson?"

Dale nodded.

"He let the CIA in to do their spying, to identify powerful Chinese nationals with gambling problems, who they could turn. And he's made deals with criminal organizations to shore up his funding during the economic slowdown. I just want to clear it all out."

"Seems like pretending to be a secretary is a terrible way to get anything done."

She shrugged.

"Maybe it's just my cover until I find a way to rob him from the inside."

"That might be the most honest thing you've said to me so far," Teddy said.

"If that's what you think, I'm not sure we can keep working together."

"Pardon?"

"I'm not going to tell you everything about me. And I already know you haven't told me everything about you," Dale said, letting that last part hang in the air for an uncomfortable amount of time. "But I've done what I can to show you what side I'm on. You'll have to make up your own mind about whether or not I can be trusted."

32

TEDDY WAS IN NO MOOD TO TALK WHEN HE GOT BACK TO the Golden Desert, but there were two police officers waiting for him who wouldn't take no for an answer. He didn't want them sniffing around Stone Barrington's suite, so he agreed to answer their questions down at the police station.

The police station in Macau was a bunker-style building that looked like someone had decorated a military barracks with gingerbread trim around the top. The officers led Teddy through the building as casually as possible and dumped him in a beige brick room that could have easily been an interview room from any suburban American police department. Teddy didn't have to wait long for a lanky detective wearing an ill-fitting suit to join him. The detective started talking to Teddy in fractured and awkward English before Teddy assured him he could understand questions in the man's native language.

"I don't speak it as well as I understand it, but I'm sure we'll find a way forward," Teddy said.

"Tell me about what happened at the production offices," the detective said.

Teddy wasn't sure how much the detective already knew, and he didn't want to give up any more information than was necessary, especially any information that might incriminate him further.

"I only know what I heard from my business partners. They said the triads attacked their film sets and then tried to blackmail them to make it stop."

"The film sets don't interest me. I asked about the production offices. You were there just today, I believe."

The man knew more about what Teddy had been up to than he'd anticipated. The key question was how.

"I was there with a woman, Dale Gai. Have you talked to her?"

"Officers are rounding up all of the interested parties," the detective said.

"Including Ms. Gai?"

"Let's talk about what you were doing at the production office. We've had officers patrolling that area due to complaints of attacks on the film crews. Was this your first time there?"

Teddy started to answer but held his tongue. It was the kind of question a detective asked when he already knew the answer and wanted to see how the subject would respond. Peter and Ben hadn't called the police to report the attacks, at first because they hadn't even realized the accidents around the set *were* attacks, and then because they feared the deepfake blackmail video would land them in hot water. Teddy assumed someone from the local film crew had made the calls.

"I only recently learned of the existence of this office," Teddy said.

"So that was the first time you'd been there?"

"We both know I'm not going to answer that the way you want me to."

"How do you think I want you to answer it?"

"I don't even know how many days I've been here. They all kind of bleed together. It's hard to keep track of what I've done or when I've done it."

"There are two production companies in that office, one American and one from Macau."

"I did know that, yes. I'm a producer with the American production company, Centurion Studios."

"Are you in Macau on Centurion Studios business?"

This was the question Teddy believed the detective had been building to, and Teddy wasn't sure what the best way was to answer it. Frankly, he was having trouble answering the question himself. He was helping Peter and Ben, but not strictly on Centurion Studios business—that they had been targeted by a blackmailer was personal.

"I was on my way back to Los Angeles and had a layover in Hong Kong."

"This is not Hong Kong."

"Dale Gai met me at the airport and told me I was needed in Macau."

The more he could stick to the truth, the better everything would be for everyone involved.

"Before or after you attacked her?"

Teddy smiled and leaned back away from the detective. There didn't seem to be anything this man didn't know about him. Teddy could see the traps being laid for him. He was done putting himself in a position to set them off.

"I came here voluntarily, thinking you and your associates were acting in good faith to keep your city safe and to protect those of us from outside of the country doing our part to support your economy."

"You came here voluntarily because you didn't want to make a scene in the resort where you are staying and where Dale Gai works."

"Tell me about Dale Gai," Teddy said.

"You followed a woman you don't know anything about from Hong Kong to Macau?"

Teddy shrugged. Then he had an idea. He kept a low profile in L.A. and didn't run into trouble much, but when he was around the police, he found his work in the film industry afforded him a certain status. He'd once heard someone refer to Hollywood celebrities as the American version of royalty, and he believed it every time he saw how everyday people reacted when they heard he worked in movies. He wondered if the same was true of the police in Macau.

"She told me she'd come on behalf of Centurion. She mentioned the film festival, and that my help was needed," Teddy said.

It seemed to work. The detective put his pen down and scratched at his right earlobe. Teddy also saw the flicker of a smile developing in a corner of the detective's mouth.

"They have a movie about a gangster showing at that festival. Maybe they should also have a movie about police officers," the detective said.

"Yes, maybe they should," Teddy said. "I really do need to get back to work with the festival. Is there anything else I can help with?"

"We know where to find you if anything comes up."

33

ARROW DONALDSON SPENT THE MORNING REGRETTING HIS involvement with Li Feng. He had known it would be risky to make a deal with her, to have her lie about her family and the Chinese government spying on the U.S. But he'd thought the risk would be from her family or the government, not from some two-bit Hollywood producer and a has-been gangster.

His original arrangement with Li Feng had been to get her a new identity and authentic papers so she could go to the U.S. and become famous as an actress or something. He'd never really bothered to ask her about it, because he didn't care. This thing with Sonny Ma was tacked on to their deal, again without him paying too much attention to the specifics, and he figured it was something Ziggy Peng would handle quickly before the government delegation showed up in Macau. Now he was on his way to his stadium to meet with that delegation, to wow them with his power and his plan to remake the rural telecom market in the U.S. And all he could think about was how much he wished Billy Barnett and Sonny Ma were dead.

The delegates were already in the owner's suite when he arrived, and his assistant mumbled something about diplomatic immunity with a shell-shocked look on her face before she scurried away.

"Gentlemen, I see you found your way to what will soon be the crown jewel of my empire in Macau and, hopefully, a gateway toward an even more advantageous relationship between Macau and the U.S."

"Cut the crap, Arrow," Bob Allen, the head of the FCC said, stepping forward. "We heard the Chinese girl was killed."

"No, no, you're mistaken. Li Feng is safe and sound in a protected bunker I arranged for her during our business here."

"We had a meeting with the CIA this morning. We know she's dead. The inspector general of the CIA was investigating the agent in charge of the operation before the FBI stepped in and took over the case."

"The FBI? I don't even know what to say to that. This is China, they have no jurisdiction here."

"Something about a drone stolen from a U.S. defense contractor that was hacked through a U.S. computer server. All I know is an FBI agent showed up at a warehouse you own with a letter from the president of the

United States giving them jurisdiction over the murder of a woman we are supposed to interview! Worse, we had to hear about it from a secretary at the CIA."

"Millie Martindale," Arrow said through clenched teeth.

"What else do you know that you haven't shared with us?"

"She's not a secretary. She works with Lance Cabot, the director of the CIA, on special projects."

"Good for her. That still doesn't answer the question of why you didn't tell us about this murder."

Arrow took a deep breath, silently went to the bar, and poured himself the largest drink he could without seeming desperate. He took a long gulp before returning to the group.

"I apologize for the confusion," Arrow said. "This is a unique case and one that was put together quickly with as few people as possible knowing all of the details to maintain the witness's safety."

"You've told us that before. Get to the murder."

"To help maintain Li Feng's security, we used a decoy to move around town and deflect attention while we moved the real Li Feng into my secure bunker. Millie Martindale had the approval of Lance Cabot to handle the operation, so I trusted her and her agency and gave them control over the security of the decoy. Perhaps I was naïve given previous issues with how U.S. intelligence agencies have operated over here, but I thought Lance Cabot and I had built a better relationship than others in the past."

Arrow knew that playing to the failures of the U.S. intelligence community was a fast-track to sympathy with this group, and it worked. Their murmurs of anger and frustration morphed into supportive nods and mumbles of camaraderie.

"I understand this has been a trying time for you, Arrow," Allen said, "but you have to understand the position a dead girl puts all of us in."

"It was never my intent to put any of you in an uncomfortable situation. The good news is that the woman you are scheduled to interview tomorrow, the woman all of you came here to meet, is still alive and under the protection of the best private security money can buy. There is certainly a place for limited governmental involvement in things like this, but I think recent events have shown that there really is no substitute for private industry."

Before anyone in the group could think too long about what they'd heard, Arrow topped off all of their drinks, rounded up the most attractive women working in the office adjacent to the construction site, and whisked them all off on a tour of what he called the "cathedral to American-Sino relations through the religion of basketball."

When the tour was done and the government delegation sufficiently inebriated and driven back to their hotel, Arrow flopped into his office chair and called his secret weapon in Hong Kong.

34

LI FENG WAS GETTING RESTLESS IN THE BUNKER. SHE FELT more like Arrow Donaldson's hostage than an asset. After his last phone call, she saw that Arrow was angry and tried to talk to him. He turned out to be surprisingly interested in her thoughts, and as they chatted, he told her about Bingo and what happened with her decoy.

As they talked, the realization dawned on her that, while Arrow Donaldson was just as powerful in Macau as he claimed to be, if not more, his influence in the U.S. was much less than he'd claimed. Since her ultimate goal was to get to the United States, her continued involvement with Arrow Donaldson worried her. Once the business with Sonny Ma was settled, she'd have to look at other options for escape in case Arrow's plans crumbled.

Now Arrow had been gone more than a day and she

was ready to break out. He'd given her a brief tour of the underground apartment when they'd first arrived, and then he'd just as quickly disappeared again. He'd phoned a couple of times and been by to visit once, but other than that she had been left alone with nothing but a television that wasn't connected to satellite TV and a computer that wasn't connected to the Internet. There were plenty of puzzles and a nicely stocked library, but she was neither an old woman nor an eccentric student, so those options didn't please her. The puzzle she was most interested in solving was how to get out of the bunker.

There was one entrance and it was dual protected with a key that Arrow carried and a code typed into a keypad. The first time Arrow left her alone after dropping her off, she had tried the door handle to test if the key and code were only needed to enter from the outside. No luck. She was locked in. The code was easy enough to figure out, even for someone like her who wasn't the most observant person in a room, but the physical key was going to be harder to come by. As far as she knew, Arrow had the only one.

She didn't want to be the kind of person who would fake sexual interest in a man to try and steal something from him. Even if Arrow found her sexually attractive, which she doubted based on his limited interactions with her, she didn't have the skills or coordination to get the key without him noticing. Smacking Arrow on the head with one of the heavy pans in the kitchen was much more her style, but she worried she would hit him too hard and kill him, which would complicate things more than she was prepared for.

Her luck turned when she had a visitor other than Arrow. She was in the kitchen cleaning up after lunch when she heard the clicking and beeping sounds of the door disarming and opening. She rushed out of the kitchen to see if there was a chance she could get past Arrow before the door relocked, but it wasn't Arrow standing in the doorway. It was his driver.

Li Feng looked down at the pan in her hand she'd been cleaning when she heard the door open. The driver obviously had a key, and she could hit him as hard as she wanted without complicating things—he was a nobody. She made a run at him before she could change her mind, and swung the pan at his head.

The next thing she knew, she was on the floor looking up at the driver, who was standing over her holding the pan in his hand.

"Did you disarm me?" she asked.

"You tripped."

"What?" She was in a daze, but looking more lucid—and more angry—every second.

"I'm sorry," he said, laughing, "I just keep replaying it in my head. You tripped on the rug there, went flying, and landed on the floor, and then the pan knocked you right on the head like some kind of cartoon."

"You didn't attack me?"

"No. But it doesn't seem like I can say the same for you."

"I guess not," she said. "I'm sorry. It was a spur-of-the-moment decision."

"Care to talk about it?"

"I feel like a hostage here. I know it's for my own protection, and I'm used to living under intense security, but this is . . . ridiculous."

"I told him you wouldn't appreciate this, and that he was making a mistake keeping you pent up."

"Really?"

"I'm not as dumb as I look. It's why Arrow finds me useful. I'm a terrible driver, but I'm good at other things."

"Like keeping women locked in a bunker?"

"That's not fair. You're the only other person he's had stay here other than himself."

"Oh," Li Feng said.

"If you really want to get out of here, though, I can help."

"That sounds like a trap."

"I don't get the chance to prove Arrow Donaldson wrong very often. This seems like quite a win for me on that front."

"You'll let me out of here? Just to get back at your boss?"

"Arrow Donaldson is your ticket to America, and I trust you recognize that your options are few. Leave me a way to get ahold of you so I can 'find' you later when he really needs you. Just don't get kidnapped or killed in the meantime."

She gave him her cell phone number and hugged him, then left the bunker. It didn't take long for her to realize that not getting kidnapped or killed was going to be harder than she thought. She was easily recognizable, and her family had probably already put out word that she was on the loose, which was the main reason she'd needed Arrow's help in Macau. But she had to get out of that bunker, and part of her wanted to witness Sonny Ma's fall from grace in person.

Arrow had mentioned the film festival and this producer named Billy Barnett who was causing trouble. Both seemed to be linked to the Golden Desert Casino and Resort that Arrow owned. Maybe Billy Barnett could help her.

35

FREED FROM THE OIG INVESTIGATION, MILLIE WANTED TO get back to keeping an eye on Arrow Donaldson, and find out what he was doing with the real Li Feng. She pushed back repeatedly on Quentin's overtures toward staying in town longer and spending more time with her, but he was persistent.

"Let's take the personal piece of it off the table. Say I don't even want to see you or spend time with you. We both still have a case to investigate."

"That's a weird way to refer to sleeping together," Millie said.

"The woman who died may not have been the woman you thought you were protecting, but someone still died, and it's still my job to find out what happened to her.

Plus, finding out who she is might help you with whatever it is you've been sent here to work on."

"That's a fair point."

"I should have known better than to appeal to you on a personal level in the first place," Quentin said jokingly. "Appealing to your work instincts is always a better path to your heart."

Millie didn't want to go back to the hotel where she'd been staying. She needed more room to spread out her investigation materials than the tiny economy room the government paid for offered, and frankly she didn't want to be under the watchful eye of the government delegation, either. Quentin's bosses hadn't planned on him being in town long enough to book a room, so she made a few calls and opened up one of the CIA safe houses in the city and told Quentin he could join her if he didn't mind sharing jurisdiction.

"It sounds so dirty when you say it like that," he said.

"Wait until you hear me talk about legal attachés."

"That just sounds like boring briefcase shopping."

The safe house was on the far edge of Coloane Village in a rural family-centric area near the beach. Millie and Quentin had both spent too much time recently in the gloom of D.C., so even though the temperature was on the cold side, they took two chairs from the safe house and dragged them out to the beach for a couple hours. When they felt they'd achieved sufficient UV-ray exposure, they ventured back inside looking for food and technology.

Quentin worked on food and dinner, while Millie worked on finding out how capable the technology was in the safe house. By the time they reconvened in the dining room an hour later, Quentin had managed to put together a meal of stewed pork and shrimp paste with egg tarts for dessert, and Millie had connected her laptop through the house's secure network to the CIA and FBI internal databases.

"It's really amazing how far you've come with the Agency," Quentin said as she showed off her handiwork. "I forget sometimes that you don't need me as much as you used to."

She looked up and smiled at Quentin with an edge that she hoped conveyed her interest in friendly conversation as long as it wasn't about her future with the CIA. He took the cue and they got through dinner pleasantly enough. Then they took their egg tarts to the office to start digging up what they could find on the Li Feng decoy.

"These taste a lot like the custard tarts my roommate used to get when I studied in London," Millie said.

She nibbled on her tart and smiled broadly. It was nice to have someone to eat with and talk with who understood, to a certain degree, what her life was like.

"I have a confession," Quentin said.

Millie expected him to offer up details about his own life experiences that she wasn't disinterested in, but she wasn't ready for the intimacy that sharing things like that always seemed to bring. But he subverted her expectations and didn't share any such thing.

"I didn't make the tarts myself. There was a box of them in the pantry and I just toasted them in the oven."

Millie couldn't hold back her laugh and wrapped her arms around him in a hug that was the closest human contact she'd had in a while. She pulled away just as quickly and started signing into the databases.

A quick check on the woman's fingerprints brought up her name as Lilly Dang and a home address in Los Angeles. It also brought up a fairly substantial rap sheet for drug and prostitution charges. While Millie finished her egg tart, Quentin took the laptop and plugged in the addresses of the woman's last few arrests.

"Seems like she spent a lot of time getting arrested near Arrow Donaldson's basketball arena," he said.

"It's probably not a stretch to assume she got in trouble once or twice with a player on Arrow Donaldson's basketball team."

"So maybe he makes some of her charges go away to keep his guy out of trouble, but then she owes Arrow a favor."

"And he asks her to come to Macau with him and stay in a luxury penthouse and live the high life for a bit while pretending to be some big-shot Chinese government witness."

"But why?" Quentin asked. "He already had his witness in Macau. Why did he need a decoy?"

"He wants to keep the real Li Feng away from us for some reason. Probably because she knows things she shouldn't, and he doesn't want her to accidentally let anything slip."

"What kinds of things would she know?"

Millie looked up and gave Quentin the most genuine

smile she could offer and said, "That's what I'm in Macau to find out."

Her phone buzzed with an incoming alert. She pushed her laptop back to Quentin while she looked at her phone. Arrow Donaldson was on his way to Hong Kong. She took her phone into the bedroom and called a man she knew very little about and said, "Arrow Donaldson is on his way to Hong Kong a day early."

36

TEDDY FAY HUNG UP WITH MILLIE MARTINDALE AND POURED himself another glass of water from the hotel suite's bar. Normally he wouldn't have cared at all when or where Arrow Donaldson traveled, but something rotten was happening in Macau and it seemed to center on Arrow Donaldson and his resort. If Donaldson was going to Hong Kong and the CIA saw that as enough of a flag to contact him, then Teddy knew where he needed to be: Hong Kong.

First, he wanted to talk to Sonny Ma. Li Feng was a moving target with too many layers of political nonsense around her to be useful for Teddy. Teddy had no interest in what she was doing for the CIA or Arrow Donaldson; all he wanted was to find out who had tried to frame and blackmail Ben and Peter. After he'd made the perpetrators pay for their wrongdoing, he could get back to L.A. in time to take a few days rest before starting his next project.

Someone was going to a lot of trouble to make it look like Sonny Ma was the one behind it, but a man like Sonny Ma would have made a lot of enemies during the course of his criminal career. Maybe the man would have an idea about who was trying to set him up. Teddy didn't know where to find Sonny Ma, but he didn't think it would be too hard for a man with his skills and experience. So far Teddy had tried to stay away from the film festival part of the business as much as possible, so that Peter and Ben's good work wouldn't be tainted by Teddy's unorthodox methods. But now that they were back in the U.S. and someone had burned down their production offices in Macau, he was already down the rabbit hole.

So instead of running around Macau trying to track down friends and family of Sonny Ma and hoping to get lucky, Teddy went to the organizing offices of the film festival where someone certainly would know how to reach the man who was the shining star of the closing night showing and benefit.

The concierge looked as if she were straight out of central casting. Teddy matched her confident and friendly smile with his own as he approached and handed her one of his Centurion Studios business cards.

"I'm Billy Barnett and I have a meeting with the film festival people here, but I can't for the life of me remember where I'm supposed to go."

"We're so excited to have all of you in our wonderful establishment for the festival," she said in clear English.

"I'm excited myself to meet Sonny Ma," Teddy said. "Is he with the rest of the organization's quarters or is he—"

"Seventeenth floor," she said, her tone turning brusque. "They have the whole floor."

It seemed Li Feng wasn't Sonny Ma's only detractor in town. Teddy slipped her a bill from his tip stash.

"Thank you. I'm sure I can find my way from there."

◆ ◆ ◆

The suite of rooms the festival occupied were as bland as Teddy had expected they would be. He'd been in hundreds of these kinds of suites in multiple countries on multiple continents, and in every case the hospitality and business suites had the same banal executive scheme.

"Good. You're here," Dale Gai said, popping her head out of one of the doors at the far end of the suite. "I wondered how long it would take."

Teddy blinked for a moment. "Nobody knew I was coming here," Teddy said. He was more than a little irritated at finding himself one step behind this woman yet again.

Dale waved him in and pointed to a large dining table where the festival organizers were congregated.

"You might fool most people as unpredictable or stealthy," she said, pouring him a drink from the bar set at the back of the room. "But to someone who isn't distracted by your flash or your . . . image, you're quite predictable."

"I need to find out who this 'someone' is."

She laughed as she handed him the drink. They sat down next to each other at the end of the table, opposite the organizers. Across from them were three women and two men, all but one of them Asian. Dale introduced Teddy and then motioned for him to talk when it was his turn.

"I need to meet with Sonny Ma," Teddy said, watching their reactions as he talked to gauge how much of the truth he needed to give them to get what he needed.

"You're with Centurion Studios," said a tall woman in a pale yellow suit and comically large glasses.

"Yes. I work with Peter and Ben."

"Who are now back in the U.S.," the two men said, almost at the same time.

This was great. It seemed like they were hoping Teddy could fill in for Peter and Ben. Teddy could work with that.

"Right. Something came up and they had to go back. I was in Hong Kong and they asked me if I could come over and help."

"You were in Hong Kong making a movie?" the woman in the suit asked.

"I was on a layover. Waiting to fly back to the U.S. Just scouting locations all over for Peter and Ben."

"You mentioned something about talking with Sonny Ma," Dale said.

He cocked an eyebrow at her, then turned back to the others.

"He's very important to this event, and I know he was very important to Peter and Ben. I want to make sure he feels taken care of."

"Very good," the woman in the suit said. The others nodded. "That's what we were hoping to hear. Dale Gai will take you to the room where he is waiting to talk to you."

"Oh she will now, will she?"

The organizers all looked at each other, confused. Teddy wondered if he'd just undone all of the good work, but Dale quickly jumped in and ended the meeting amicably before Teddy could ruin it any further. He kept his composure and managed to wait until they were well out of earshot of the others before he stopped her and asked her what she'd been up to after she left him alone to deal with the police about the burning production office.

"That's none of your business, and I couldn't tell you the truth even if I wanted to," she said.

37

THE FIRST THING TEDDY NOTICED WHEN SONNY MA OPENED the door to his suite was that he was enormous. He filled nearly the entire doorway. The second thing he noticed was that Dale didn't seem surprised at all. She knew more about Sonny Ma than she'd let on. Teddy was frustrated that he still found himself breaking down her every move and her every word, comparing himself to her or analyzing her actions. When this was all over, he was looking forward to getting back to L.A. where he more rarely had trouble separating friend from foe.

Dale made the introductions and Sonny Ma welcomed them into the suite. Teddy had been in the homes and hotel rooms of powerful and dangerous people who had no trouble feigning kindness and generosity, but

Teddy was caught off guard by Sonny Ma's seemingly genuine openness. And it wasn't just directed at Dale.

"Peter and Ben were so great here for the city," Sonny said to Teddy, handing him a glass of Chinese whiskey. "I hope we can find a way for you to do the same."

Teddy took the drink, a dark amber color rather than the traditionally clear Chinese *baijiu*, and toasted their host.

"I'd love to have a bottle of this sent to my friend Stone Barrington," Teddy said. "Peter's father. What is it?"

"It's a new whiskey, created and distilled in Scotland, then aged here in ancient clay pots instead of wooden barrels. I'll have a bottle sent to your room."

Teddy had no doubt that Sonny Ma would get the bottle to the right room without any further information from Teddy. He took another drink and then another before slowing his sips and sitting down in an ornamental chair across from the small matching couch where Dale and Sonny sat.

"I hope the organizers and my . . . compatriot here have let you in on the other reasons I wanted to talk with you," Teddy said.

"Other than movies and fine whiskey?"

Teddy held back a frown, not wanting to give his true motivations away before he was ready. Sonny smiled and took a large drink of his own whiskey.

"Not everyone likes me. Many want me dead. But many more want me to make another movie where I fight with swords and jump off of buildings into helicopters. No man is a star to everyone."

"Is that because you can't help getting back into the criminal game?"

"There are many things I have trouble denying myself, but criminal activity is not one of them," Sonny replied, seeming unoffended by Teddy's unsubtle probing.

"Someone is trying to make it look like you're reviving your gangster empire again."

Sonny didn't hide his frown as he reached for the whiskey decanter, passing it over for a bottle of water instead. Teddy also took a bottle of water and sipped on it as he recounted what he'd learned so far. Dale sat quietly, listening.

Teddy continued. "Can you think of who might want to set you up?"

Sonny exhaled loudly. "It is, I suspect, a woman I knew when we were younger. A woman named Li Feng."

"We suspected as much," Teddy said. "Tell us everything you can."

"Before I was a thief and a crook and then a movie star, I was a child. And I was friends with Li Feng. Our parents were important, and we went to a school where everyone's parents were important."

"How do you go from a school like that to a criminal empire?"

Sonny Ma gave Teddy a look of derision and contempt.

"The better question is how anyone who goes to a school like that *doesn't* end up running a criminal empire."

"Excellent point," Teddy said. "I guess some businesses are just more upfront than others about their criminality."

"Like Arrow Donaldson's businesses?" Sonny said. "Li Feng does not have the power on her own to wage a campaign against my reputation like this. Someone is helping her."

"Her family is quite powerful. Why could they not help her?"

"Her family is one of the most corrupt criminal empires in China, but they wish me no harm. I am a national treasure. They would ruin their own reputation by ruining mine."

"Does Arrow Donaldson have any reason to hate you?"

Sonny Ma shrugged.

"I told you already that many men hate me. Arrow Donaldson may be one of them."

"This doesn't seem to worry you much," Teddy said. "Under normal circumstances I would bid you a fond farewell and go on my way, leaving you to fight your own battles."

"I am very capable of fighting any battles I choose," Sonny said.

"But this battle between you and Li Feng has dragged two of my friends into it. I have assured them I will make those responsible pay for what they've done."

Teddy's and Sonny's gazes were locked on each other until Dale spoke for the first time in this conversation.

"You two are making this harder and stupider than it needs to be. You don't have to fight against each other to protect your reputations or to get revenge. Just fight your own battles and keep each other informed."

Teddy nodded, looking at Dale. He was grateful for her calming nature. And because her skills hinted at experiences close to his own, he could trust that she was making her suggestions strategically and not just to placate him. It was the same thing he had done for others, including the president of the United States, in similar circumstances.

"She's right," Teddy said. "I won't get in your way, and there doesn't seem to be any reason for you to get in mine. But if either of us hears of anything that could help the other, we'll share it as quickly as possible."

"I can drink to that. And it seems I may need to send a bottle of this whiskey to you as well, Dale Gai."

"I won't turn down any gifts," she said, "but I'll just be happy with fewer men killing each other in my streets."

38

TEDDY AND DALE WERE QUIET ON THE WALK BACK TO STONE Barrington's suite. The conversation with Sonny Ma had been a good one. Teddy felt on top of what was going on in Macau for the first time since he'd arrived. His last conversation with Dale, though, had not been a good one, and the discomfort hung heavy in the air between them.

"I'm sorry for not trusting you," he said.

She ignored him and hit the button for the elevator to the penthouse level. Teddy held back from saying anything else or pushing for a response as they waited for the elevator to descend.

When they were inside the elevator, she finally said, "You're not what I expected and that's been hard to deal with."

At first Teddy thought she meant his looks or his personality. He held his tongue and let her continue speaking, which proved a wise move.

"I'm the best at what I do around here, and I like that," she said.

"Security? Right?"

"All of it—security, rescue, investigation. I feel like I've developed an alternative to all of the shadow operations in this city meant to harm people and prop up the rich."

"That sounds a lot like what I do back in L.A. for the people around me."

She didn't say anything about that not being the job of a movie producer, but at this point, Teddy suspected she knew everything she needed to about him. He wouldn't even be surprised if she knew his real name.

"This thing with Arrow and Li Feng was part of that, and I thought I was doing a good job. Peter and Ben needed my help and I thought I could take care of it all."

"Then they wanted to bring me in," Teddy said.

The door opened at their floor, but neither of them got off the elevator. After several seconds of inactivity, the door closed, and the elevator went back down.

"I thought they wanted you to help them with the festival or with their film projects since they were distracted by the attacks and the fake videos."

"What did they tell you about me, exactly?" Teddy said.

"They called you a troubleshooter and said you had special skills that were perfect for this kind of situation.

In retrospect it sounds exactly like they were bringing you in to take out the bad guys, but who would have thought nice guy movie producers knew people like that?"

"You met Stone Barrington, right?"

"Yes. He's the one who seemed like the big-shot fixer. When he left town, I assumed you would take over the production stuff, and I would help them find the bad guys."

"And you have. You've just done it with me instead of on your own."

"I don't normally work well with others," she said.

"Me, either," Teddy said.

She smiled and Teddy could feel the awkwardness in the air lift. They both reached for the button to take them back up to the penthouse at the same time.

Teddy was ready to continue the conversation and develop a plan of attack with Dale, but as they exited the elevator onto the penthouse floor, they were stopped by a cluster of police surrounding the elevator.

"You're under arrest for the murder of Zhou Peng," one of the uniformed officers said.

Teddy couldn't tell if he was talking to Dale or him, but he suspected it probably was meant for them both.

◆ ◆ ◆

Bingo was at the Golden Desert Casino looking for Billy Barnett when he heard a group of tourists talking about an attack on an American by a motorcycle gang. He figured it must be Gong's work, and was planning to call Gong to congratulate him on a job well done when the tone of the conversation turned.

"The American nearly beat that giant to death before he escaped," one of the tourists said.

That did not sound great, and Bingo was less inclined to reach out to Gong, who would be in a terrible mood. This whole thing was getting out of hand. Between Li Feng's grudge attacks on Sonny Ma and these American movie people blowing up everything they touched, his city was going to be destroyed if someone didn't stop them all soon. Arrow and Li Feng were busy with their complicated schemes, but Bingo knew the only way to save his city was to take them all out.

When the elevator stopped, he got off and took the stairs the rest of the way to avoid detection as much as possible. At the floor where Billy Barnett was staying, Bingo took two steps out of the stairwell before he saw the police officers. He briefly wondered if they were there for him, then he saw them taking Dale Gai and Billy Barnett away. Excellent. Two problems down, and he didn't even have to do anything.

Now he just needed to take care of Li Feng before her obsession with Sonny Ma got them all killed or arrested.

39

DALE LOOKED LIKE SHE WANTED TO ARGUE WITH THE POlice, to fight back against the arresting officers and run. Teddy was resigned to his fate and allowed himself to be handcuffed without giving the police a reason to send him away to a camp somewhere like they'd done with Bingo's family. Neither of them talked with each other or with the police.

Even with the tight handcuffs and the chains locking the cuffs to the floor of the van, it wasn't the toughest situation Teddy had found himself in. But as Teddy subtly examined the locks and tested his maneuverability, Dale sat unmoving and uninterested. She didn't seem to have any interest in even trying to escape.

"After our conversation in the elevator I would have

expected this to be our moment to shine together," Teddy said.

"And make it worse? We should have cleaned up better after killing him. I should have cleaned up better after killing him. I know better than that."

"Are you implying that I don't know better or that this is my fault?" Teddy asked.

"I'm not implying anything. No, I don't think this is your fault. This whole thing has been sideways from the beginning and everything I do, everything *we* do, makes it worse."

"It only seems that way because we're skilled enough to dig deep, to show that what seemed simple at first is even more complex and corrupt than we expected. It's the curse of our particular skill set."

"It seems a lot like failure," Dale said.

"Maybe that's where working in the movie business has given me some perspective. If it weren't for successes that seem like failures in the movie business, I wouldn't have any success at all. You have to work hard for every scrap, and so many times the effort isn't worth the reward. But that's making movies. This is saving people."

"Who are we saving? Peter and Ben are already back in the U.S. The police will probably send you back, too, and close down the film festival, and you'll be okay while I'm left here to take the brunt of the fallout."

"I won't let that happen," Teddy said.

The van stopped before the conversation could continue and two officers came around to the back to unhook them from the floor and take them into the station. Instead of going through the front entrance and heading to the interview rooms, as he'd done on his last visit to the police station, he and Dale were led through the back entrance into the booking area with the street criminals and hooligans.

Teddy turned to find Dale, but she was already gone, being led out a different door. Despite his encouraging words, privately Teddy admitted to himself that Dale was right: this was starting to feel like failure. But as soon as he was about to trade optimism for pessimism, he saw an opportunity developing. He was dumped into a holding cell, and the arresting uniformed officers were replaced with two other uniformed officers who just so happened to be the cops he'd talked to earlier after the production office fire. They had seemed very interested in the movie business.

"Hey there, remember me?" Teddy asked the officer facing him.

"Mr. Big Man Movie Producer. I remember you. Looks like maybe you're living out too many scenes from a movie in real life."

"Life has certainly gotten complicated," Teddy said. "It's all a big misunderstanding, of course, and I'm sure it'll be sorted out when all the lawyers and powers that be get together. In the meantime, I wondered if you might be able to help me with a phone call I need to make."

"You movie people! Your films spread that stuff about guaranteed phone calls in jail—nowadays everyone arrested starts whining about their phone call and their rights. It's a courtesy in *both* countries, applied at the discretion of the jail staff." This was obviously a sore point for the officer.

"Can I hope for your discretion in this matter?" Teddy asked.

"Need to make some kind of big-time movie phone call?"

"The movie business doesn't shut down just because one of the producers gets caught up in some foreign drama," Teddy said.

The cop was nodding along as he headed toward the cell, taking out the swipe card that would open Teddy's cell.

"These sorts of things might not happen to you as much if you had some local police on your set to keep everyone safe and keep those lines of communication open with those powers that be."

Teddy couldn't tell if the guy was angling for a legitimate change in career or if he was looking for some kind of juiced up fake position that amounted to a bribe, but Teddy made sure the cop knew he would help any way he could. The officer handed Teddy an older model flip phone, then disappeared. Teddy dialed Millie, hoping she wouldn't ignore a call from an unknown number.

After two rings, she answered. "This is Millie."

"I need your help."

She paused. "I feel like a bartender with a tab that's never going to be paid."

"People like us, in this business, we're family. You want to help family, right?"

"That would make you the weird uncle that only shows up once in a while, right?"

"I'd make a *Man from U.N.C.L.E.* joke, but I feel like it would be wasted on someone your age."

"Just get to the favor, old man."

"I need you to convince Arrow Donaldson to bail me out of jail," Teddy said.

Millie made a choking sound on the other end of the line and took a second to recover before speaking.

"Your faith in me is heartening."

"My faith in you is situational. You know what to do."

40

LI FENG THOUGHT SHE KNEW MACAU. SHE REALIZED quickly that she held the naïve perspective of the pampered daughter of a wealthy family and an executive of a powerful company. Being driven around in a car and escorted by security was different from navigating in the shadows on her own. Still, she'd managed not only to find Billy Barnett, the film producer who had given Arrow Donaldson so much headache, but to follow him undetected.

She first found him by accident when she went looking for Kwok Lin, an old fool who imagined himself as some kind of movie industry strong man, but who also was known to hoard street gossip, especially related to out-of-towners and tourists. Luckily, she didn't have to listen to him sing karaoke at the bar he'd adopted as his office. As she arrived, she saw an American leaving with a Chinese woman she recognized as a security assistant from Arrow Donaldson's casino.

Suspecting this man was Billy Barnett, she followed him to be certain. Her suspicion was confirmed when he went from the karaoke bar to an office that turned out to be a film production office. When Billy Barnett left the office and went back to the casino, she had planned to approach him to ask for help. She stopped herself because of the security assistant from the casino. Why were they together? Maybe Billy Barnett wasn't the right person to help protect her from Arrow after all. She needed more time to think.

With nowhere to sleep or shelter that night, she broke back into the secure bunker with the code the driver had given her, then left the security pad disabled so she could come and go as she pleased. The next morning, her course of action was decided. She would confront Sonny Ma on her own, and kill him instead of having others do it for her. Sneaking around in the shadows, hiding and trying to disguise herself, had reignited her dormant criminal instincts. She craved more. There was no way she could get to Sonny Ma on Arrow Donaldson's turf, so she stayed in the shadows and watched for a moment of weakness she could exploit.

41

MILLIE WAS AT THE MACAU BUSINESS AVIATION CENTER saying goodbye to Quentin when she got a call from her mystery man. Despite their banter, he really wasn't a mystery to her, but she didn't let anyone know how much she was aware of his background. She'd been working in the president's national security office when she'd met the man for the first time. He'd called himself Fred Walker, and though she'd known right away that the name was fake, she hadn't asked any questions.

Fred Walker had wanted her to go undercover to help him with a mission for the president. It had turned out to be pretty exciting, even if she hadn't realized how much she craved the excitement at the time. She received credit for killing a terrorist, though in truth that had been accomplished by her mysterious colleague. But her new reputation for keeping cool in the line of fire got her moved over to the CIA director's office, where Fred Walker came calling again. By that time, she'd found her unrealized desire for adventure and an outlet for her natural curiosity. She wasn't going to let Fred Walker go unchecked a second time. She still didn't know his real name, but she knew his main identity was as movie producer Billy Barnett, and she had suspicions that he also occasionally used the alias of Mark Weldon to do stunt work and character acting.

From working with Lance, she'd also managed to deduce that Fred/Billy/Mark had once been one of the most wanted men in the country. He'd done something terrible and then redeemed himself by doing something equally terrible, but for the right team this time.

Now he was calling her to ask another favor. She looked forward to one day calling in all of his favors, but for the time being she listened to his quick burst of conversation before he hung up. It only took her a few seconds to come up with a way to help her mystery man, and to let Arrow know she was on to him. Two birds with one stone.

Arrow answered her call after the first ring. Millie smiled to herself. He could complain about her all he wanted, but he knew she still held some pull with Lance, who was the key to the whole operation succeeding.

"I know you're going to Hong Kong early, but there's someone here in jail in Macau who could be an asset to you if you can get him out."

Arrow's frustration was almost palpable, even over the

phone. He had decidedly *not* told her about his upcoming trip. "I find it hard to believe you've had enough time away from questioning by your agency to spy on me," he said.

"I'm in intelligence. It's my job to absorb as much information as possible from as many different sources and about as many different people as I can."

"Your time is wasted if you're spying on your friends rather than enemies."

"This man is a known troublemaker. *He's* the one I'm spying on. I don't trust him, and I don't believe his presence here—at this exact time—is a coincidence."

"You think he's here to kill Li Feng?"

"Maybe. I'd really like to find out, but he won't talk to me." Millie put a tone of frustration into her voice to imply that Billy Barnett wouldn't deal with a young woman like her. Totally untrue, but Arrow had no way of knowing that, and would interpret the situation according to his own biases.

"I'm starting to like this guy already. What's his name?"

Millie paused as dramatically as possible before she said, "Billy Barnett."

◆ ◆ ◆

Arrow tried not to choke when the girl from the CIA asked him to bail Billy Barnett out of jail. His first thought was to find someone in the jail he could bribe to kill the meddlesome producer, but that would expend almost all of the political capital he'd built up in the region. He didn't want to waste it on some lowlife producer.

But this lowlife producer had shown a knack for violent problem solving. Arrow wondered if it wouldn't be a good idea to try to get Billy Barnett on his side. In the worst case, Barnett turned down an alliance, and Arrow could kill him and pin it on Sonny Ma. Or even better, if Billy Barnett was already known to the CIA, Arrow could get rid of Li Feng and frame Barnett. The mess with Sonny Ma had blown up out of proportion. Li Feng had become more trouble than her testimony was worth.

Arrow called his secret weapon in Hong Kong to say that he would be running late and to continue planning their next move until he arrived. Then he went to the Macau public safety building to bail Billy Barnett out of jail.

42

ARROW BRIEFLY WONDERED HOW HE WOULD BE RECEIVED by the Macau police. He never worried that they weren't in his pocket or on his side, but the nature of Ziggy Peng's work for him had occasionally put Ziggy into conflict with them. Would their investigation of his murder be used to dig up dirt on Arrow that they could use later against him, or use to increase their bribery fees? Had they arrested Billy Barnett knowing the man was of interest to Arrow?

His worries were quickly put aside when he was greeted at the door by the secretariat for security himself. Arrow had called his casino security people to find out what had happened during the arrest, and then had his interim security chief call the police station and let them know he was on his way. The chief was conciliatory and apologetic that one of Arrow's men had been killed under their watch.

"That's very kind of you," Arrow said, taking a seat in the pale green office of the public safety director. "I appreciate your concern during this difficult time."

"We were very concerned to hear that this man had been murdered in his own hotel by one of his own assistants and a movie producer from the United States."

"As was I," Arrow said. "I've been handling some very important business with some VIP guests in town and I assumed I could leave my security needs in the care of Zhou Peng."

Arrow could see the secretariat's face swell with curiosity when he heard the mention of VIP guests, and Arrow made a mental note to keep his activities related to the testimony even closer to his vest than normal. The last thing he needed was a curious police executive nosing around and scaring the U.S. government delegation even further.

"What kind of VIP guests?"

"We have many VIPs at the Golden Desert," Arrow said quickly. "It's why my business is so important to this country, and why the security of my property is paramount."

"We will make sure that the two killers are punished to the fullest extent."

"I appreciate your diligence in this matter," Arrow said. "But in the case of the movie producer, his stature, along with his status as a U.S. citizen, brings some complications. I'd like to deal with him myself."

The secretariat was losing his patience and his attention span was beginning to wander. It seemed Arrow had ruined the mood by not letting them take Billy Barnett and hang him in the public square as an example.

"We don't usually hand over murder suspects to private citizens."

Arrow put on his most somber face and leaned in closer to the man.

"Between you and me, man-to-man, I think we only have one murder suspect here. This woman, Dale Gai, was sneaking around Zhou Peng's back. And I have reason to believe she was not loyal to me or my interests in this country. This movie producer was just another dumb American blinded by a woman, and I'd hate to see him suffer for that bad choice."

"You can take the movie producer away from here now. The woman stays."

"I understand," Arrow said.

They finished off the conversation with pleasantries and empty promises to keep in touch with each other about their operations. then Arrow went to meet Billy Barnett for the first time.

43

ARROW DONALDSON WAS JUST ABOUT THE LAST PERSON Teddy would have expected to be bailing him out of jail. It was a most interesting turn of events. The casino mogul was joined by the secretariat of security to transfer Teddy from the jail to Arrow's waiting car. Teddy got in first without hesitation. He wanted to project confidence and trust, knowing a man like Arrow Donaldson would feed on any hint of fear. Arrow got in after Teddy and asked the driver for a drink.

The driver handed back a flask, which Arrow in turn offered to Teddy as they drove away. "Need a pick-me-up? Sounds like it's been a rough day for you."

"Jail is certainly never easy."

"You've been in jail before?" Arrow asked.

Teddy could almost see the man laying the trap. If Arrow wanted to learn more about Billy Barnett, Teddy was happy to oblige. He took the drink Arrow offered, and said, "Not like this, no. We've done filming in jails before and I've done research, you know, but not like that, no. Wow."

Teddy took another drink and flopped back in his seat. "This is a nice car," Teddy said, looking around like he was assessing the vehicle's amenities rather than looking for anything he could use as a weapon if this turned out to be a trap.

Arrow ignored that comment, shifting instead to the business at hand. "I'm glad I could help you out of a sticky situation."

Teddy sat up, as if recalling his manners. "I can't tell you how much I appreciate your help. I'm sure the police enjoyed having a high-profile American in custody, and may have been reluctant to let go of their prize."

Arrow nodded. Teddy sensed he was putting out the right vibes as the reckless rich American Arrow expected him to be.

Teddy continued, "Now that unpleasantness is past, I'm looking forward to being elbow-deep in a pile of chips at the craps table."

"There is no greater luxury than having enough money to waste it on something exciting," Arrow said. Then after a brief pause, he finished with, "And dangerous."

"You know something I don't about the craps table at your place?"

Arrow took a drink directly from the flask this time, and handed it back to Teddy who followed with his own long swig.

"A true gamble can't be had at a table, my friend."

"You got something in mind, spit it out, *friend*," Teddy said.

"It's just all so . . . glossy. So boring."

The inflections in his voice and his body language seemed genuine to Teddy. He wondered if something about being buzzed in the back of a car together was creating a spark of bonding between them.

As Arrow finished the rest of the alcohol in the flask, Teddy realized Dale Gai wasn't with them. Maybe she'd been released on her own and was at the casino waiting for them.

"Dale Gai was arrested with me," Teddy said, taking advantage of their new bond as they approached the hotel entrance. "You may know her. She works at the casino in security. She was assisting me with security for the film festival."

"I can't be expected to know every employee. It's a large operation. I'll talk to someone in HR and make sure she's provided the resources she needs locally to defend herself."

Teddy had two paths in front of him, and neither was very good. He could push further for Dale's release and risk having Arrow send him back to jail, with prejudice, where he might not ever be seen again. Or, he could do exactly what he'd told Dale Gai he wouldn't do and sell her out to save his own skin.

In the end, the logical decision was clear, if unpalatable. Neither he nor Dale Gai would be well-served by him being locked up again. It only raised the odds that whoever was trying to destroy Peter and Ben's interests in Macau would succeed.

Dale had already shown she had survival skills comparable to Teddy's, so he had no doubt she would be fine for the time being. When the time was right, if needed, he could marshal the resources to break her out.

"You're right," Teddy said, as they exited the car at the casino's entrance. "Why put what you and I can do together at risk because of a woman."

Arrow smiled a wide, contemptable smile as he emerged from the car and escorted Teddy into the hotel as if he were an honored guest.

44

"I KNOW PEOPLE THINK I'M SOME KIND OF GLOBAL SUPER-villain," Arrow said to Teddy. "And maybe they're right. This is my lair and I can't say it does anything to dispel that impression of me. But I like it. It's secure and it gives me a place to work and think without distraction."

"Is this where you inject me with truth serum or torture me until I give up all of my secrets?"

"I'm squeamish, believe it or not, and hate torture. The results are mixed, at best, and you end up looking like a jerk. No, in fact, this is where I tell you all of my evil plans so you know how powerful I am and maybe decide to join my side."

"I've never been one to stick to a single side for very long, so let's hear your plan."

"I have many powerful friends in the U.S. government who do not care for China."

"So far so good."

"For a long time, certain government agencies were using my casinos under my nose to try and flip high-level officials with gambling problems to spy on the Chinese government."

"That sounds terrible for business," Teddy said.

"I shut it down as quickly as possible, but they wouldn't go away until I gave them something else they wanted. That's when I found Li Feng.

"She has information about massive spying by the Chinese government on U.S. citizens through the cell phone technology her family's company makes. And I've convinced her to testify in front of Congress."

"You sound like quite the hero," Teddy said. "I hate to be the one to tell you that I don't have any secrets that would be of interest to the Chinese or American governments."

"That's not what I need you for. I've been following your activities since you arrived in Macau. For a movie producer you seem to have remarkable skills at protecting your friends. You also seem to be quite discreet. I was only able to follow your activities because so many of them took place within my casino."

Teddy already had more going on in Macau than he anticipated and had no interest in palling around with Arrow Donaldson, but this seemed like the best way to find out what Arrow's involvement was in harassing Peter and Ben. He took the bait.

"I do what I can," Teddy said. "You have friends you'd like me to protect for you?"

"What I'd really like for you to do," Arrow continued, "is keep an eye on Li Feng. Discreetly. She's under my protection right now, but eventually the U.S. government will take custody of her. But I don't trust their capabilities. One woman has already died here under their watch."

Teddy could see the entire galaxy of trouble swirling around Arrow Donaldson. Peter and Ben were small pieces of something much larger, and to execute the revenge he'd promised Stone and Dino, Teddy was going to have to blow up the entire thing. Keeping an eye on Li Feng would certainly help with that, but the longer Teddy was in Macau, the more likely it was he was going to uncover something even he couldn't fix.

♦ ♦ ♦

Arrow watched Billy Barnett leave and wondered if stringing him along was the smart move. Maybe he should have just shot the movie producer right then. He sat on the edge of the desk and thought about the gun in his drawer next to the cashbox and a box of expensive cigars. He'd always been able to get what he wanted by using money and connections, and letting other people handle the violence.

Li Feng was turning out to be a curse that had already taken down some powerful men. Billy Barnett seemed less dumb and cocksure than every other L.A. suit he'd ever dealt with—and he appeared to be able to get almost as much done in Macau as Arrow. In another world, without the fate of the QuiTel ban and Arrow's future in that market at stake, he might try to team up with a man like Billy Barnett. But Arrow didn't see any reason why, once Billy Barnett went against Li Feng, he would fare any differently than the others who had crumbled.

Arrow also told himself that he would be able to use the gun and put down any interference in the biggest deal of his life, if necessary. He took the gun out of the drawer and rolled it around in his hands, familiarizing himself with the grooves and contours. Then he took out one of the cigars and lit it. The cigar was definitely better.

45

AFTER DECLINING ARROW DONALDSON'S OFFER TO PUT Teddy up in a suite of his own, Teddy retreated to Stone Barrington's suite and called Millie Martindale.

"Can you help me get in touch with the CIA lackey who told Arrow Donaldson to spring me from jail?" Teddy asked when Millie answered.

"That doesn't sound like anyone I know," Millie said.

"Even you?"

"That depends on the hour of the day and the day of the week."

"What about today?"

"I *may* have let it slip when I was talking to Arrow that you were in jail in Macau."

"And then he just took the initiative to hunt me down and spring me out all on his own?"

"He's very ambitious from what I've heard."

"Ruthless as well. The woman I was arrested with is still there and didn't receive as favorable a review as myself with Mr. Donaldson."

"Your private life doesn't concern me, Mr. Barnett."

"Not that kind of woman. More like a partner. A coworker."

"Did we ever get around to talking about why you're in Macau in the first place?" Millie asked.

"I think that's what Arrow Donaldson is trying to find out. Maybe you can ask him."

"I'm more interested in this woman."

"How progressive of you," Teddy said.

"Aside from conning me into helping you once or twice, your reputation isn't that of a man who works well with others."

"Others aren't usually as highly trained as I am."

"How well-trained does a movie producer need to be exactly?"

"I think this conversation is veering off course. I just wanted to thank whoever in your organization brought my plight to the attention of Arrow Donaldson, and let you know that he doesn't trust the U.S. delegation to provide proper security for Li Feng. He's asked me to keep an eye on her."

"Good luck with that," Millie said. "There's already been one attempt on her life, and I'm almost certain Arrow is the one who ordered it. He gave me a decoy instead of the real Li Feng—and then he killed her."

"There's a gangster named Sonny Ma that everyone in

Macau seems to believe is behind all of the bad things happening. Maybe he tried to kill her thinking it was the real Li Feng."

"Keep in touch about what you learn from your new friend Arrow Donaldson," Millie said. Then she hung up.

Teddy was growing more impressed with that young woman even as she exasperated him more and more with her bravado and spunk.

As he browsed the room service menu looking for something that sounded good to eat as a recharge meal, Teddy thought of Dale Gai. Teddy still felt guilty about leaving jail without her and needed to eat so he could do something about it. He ordered a steak, medium rare, and fries, then went the bathroom to put together another disguise while he waited for it to be delivered.

♦ ♦ ♦

The third time Teddy entered the Macau police station he had the leathery look of a veteran troublemaker and the ponytail of a man lost in time. Billy Barnett hadn't gotten very far with the police, so Teddy was giving Atticus Hackman, civil rights attorney and professional savior, a try. He had to wander around for several minutes before someone pointed him toward a small glassed-in booth with a chubby young man in a uniform, different from the police officers' uniforms, stuffed inside.

"I need to talk to Dale Gai," Teddy said.

"We don't have anyone here by that name."

"She's not an employee. She was arrested earlier today."

"We don't have anyone here by that name," the young man said again.

It was a rote response, and a lie at that. Someone had told this kid to fend off anyone looking for Dale Gai, no matter what he heard or who was asking. Teddy knew he wasn't going to get any further at the police station, so he took the opportunity to look around the station and scope out the setup. He made some mental notes and left, knowing how he would get Dale back.

46

QUENTIN WAS ON HIS WAY BACK TO D.C. AND MILLIE FELT like she could finally get back to business. She had genuinely loved seeing him. The time they spent together was amazing and heartfelt, but it was better for their relationship if they kept work separate from private matters.

She was about to leave the Macau Business Aviation Center when through the giant window she spotted a plane she recognized landing on the airstrip. It was the twin to the CIA chartered plane she'd arrived in. Her curiosity turned to cautious optimism when she recognized the man deplaning: Lance Cabot, the director of the CIA.

"Welcome to Macau, boss. Here to offer me a promotion?" she asked, trying to grab at him and push him off to the side so no one saw him. "Who knows you're here?"

"It's good to see you, too, Ms. Martindale."

She knew he wasn't there for banter or to check on her progress; he was there about the dead woman. The dead woman she still had no answer for.

"I'm working on getting to the bottom of what happened. I'm absolutely certain Arrow Donaldson was behind that women's murder. If we can prove that, then—"

"We don't investigate murders. We gather information and present that information, unbiased, to those above us who make the hard decisions about this country," Lance said.

"We had an agreement that when I arrived in Macau, security for Li Feng would be transferred to my team. Arrow Donaldson reneged on that agreement."

"You may not believe this, but I really do respect your enthusiasm for this job. That's rare in our line of work and it's refreshing."

"I'm a part of this team, a real part of this team, not the mascot. You wouldn't have put me anywhere near Arrow Donaldson if you weren't confident in my abilities on some level."

"I just wish you were more ambitious when someone needs to be sent to Siberia."

"Didn't the Agency once steal a bunch of Russian helicopters, run up a five-million-dollar bar bill, and then accidentally blow up an oil pipeline in Siberia?"

"It wasn't accidental. And how do you know about that?"

"I'm happy to sign up for stealing helicopters anywhere you want to send me."

"Where's the congressional delegation that was looking into this? I should probably make an appearance and do my government-funded schmoozing."

"Still at their hotel, last I know. Li Feng's testimony is supposed to happen at the consulate in Hong Kong where they have secure facilities. But as far as I know Arrow is the only one who's gone over to Hong Kong since I've been here."

"Did he take Li Feng with him?"

"I don't know. I haven't been able to talk to her yet."

"Go talk to the delegates and see what they think. See if you can talk them into taking you to Hong Kong early to see what Arrow's up to."

"They will. Trust me."

"I've got some other business to attend to in town, but I'll be here to offer support from the top if you need it, or to stay in the shadows if you don't."

"That's helpful and creepy. Wonderful," Millie said.

47

TEDDY DIDN'T TRUST A SINGLE WORD THAT CAME OUT OF Arrow Donaldson's mouth; he suspected Arrow felt the same way about him. As long as they both kept up the illusion that they were working with each other, there was always the chance that it could net a benefit for Teddy. It also gave him an opportunity to keep tabs on Arrow without looking too conspicuous.

But Dale Gai didn't have the luxury of waiting around while Teddy played games with Arrow. She might have already been swept away to some kind of prison camp where Teddy wouldn't be able to save her without making an international incident out of it. But he wasn't going to rest until he'd made every effort he could to prove that he wouldn't leave her behind.

When he returned to Stone Barrington's suite, he

called the festival organizers and asked if they could spare a local actress for him to use for some promo work. Jee Go showed up fifteen minutes later at Teddy's door, took his money, and let him disguise her without questions. He told her very little about what was going to happen, because he wanted her surprise and confusion to be genuine. His only preparatory comment was "You're going to have to trust me."

When they arrived at the police station, Teddy checked through his pockets to make sure he had everything he needed. Then he grabbed his decoy by the arm and dragged her to the information desk.

Teddy was happy to see that someone was behind the desk other than the fat young man who'd been there the last time. That was the first, and most important, roadblock to bypass for Teddy's plan to work. He was suddenly feeling much more confident in his success and that fed his performance for the surrounding audience of officers and bystanders.

"I've captured this escaped fugitive and risked my life to get her off the streets and I would like a reward for my effort," Teddy said, to no one in particular.

The actress looked up at him and, probably for the first time, realized her situation wasn't as rosy as she'd been led to believe. She tried to pull away and the realism was great enough that the skinny old clerk behind the glassed-in desk seemed to suddenly register what was going on.

"What did you say?" the woman asked Teddy.

"This is Dale Gai, a wanted murder suspect who escaped from your custody. I found her and have brought her back. I'd like to claim my reward."

The actress was really putting up a fight by that point, yelling in Chinese, presumably protesting Teddy's story.

The skinny old clerk was typing furiously into an old computer terminal and had a rotating look of confusion, horror, and irritation on her face. Teddy waited patiently and managed to keep his impostor under control.

"I don't show anywhere that anyone by that name has escaped," the clerk said.

"They're not going to put that kind of stuff in the computer for just anybody to find," Teddy said.

The actress continued yelling at an escalating pitch. Teddy sensed that causing a scene by getting the girl and the clerk riled up would help further his plan. It seemed to be working. The clerk looked increasingly desperate to find information to corroborate what Teddy was telling her.

She was on the phone for a few seconds screaming at someone on the other end, and then it seemed like she spent another few seconds being screamed at in turn.

"This office is supposed to be the law-and-order headquarters for this region and I spend a lot of money in Macau every year and that's going to come to an abrupt end right now if I can't be assured that murderers won't be running the streets because the police can't keep track of who's in jail and who isn't."

"I'm really sorry, sir, but Dale Gai is still in our system. I can see that her status was last updated fifteen minutes ago. It shows her still in this building."

Teddy pushed the actress forward toward the clerk.

"Tell her who you are," Teddy said.

The actress looked back at Teddy and fell silent, fuming. The clerk seemed to be at a crossroads internally.

Teddy suspected he needed a bit more of a distraction to push her over the edge into the action he needed next for his plan. Turning away from the desk, Teddy instead addressed the pockets of bystanders in the station, ranting and raving about what a scam the police were and how poorly treated he was as a foreigner and a tourist with vital money to spend in the country.

His speech didn't do much to rile up anyone looking on, and it wasn't persuasive enough for the clerk to leave her post. Teddy was analyzing the situation and evaluating possible moves. The plan had always been a long shot, and it appeared he was back to square one. Then fate intervened when a cluster of uniformed officers walked by with the real Dale Gai in tow.

"See. Right there. That's Dale Gai," the clerk said.

Before she could say anything further, Teddy used a customized shooter in his belt buckle to deploy a burst of mild tear gas in the area around Dale. That gave Teddy a brief opening to grab her and the actress each by an arm, and push them outside the police station. They were finally able to flag down a taxi a few blocks later. Dale and the actress were still coughing at even the minor irritant in the spray he'd used, but they didn't need to like him right then. They were all safe and he'd kept his word.

48

TEDDY HAD THE CAB DROP THE FILM FESTIVAL ACTRESS OFF at the casino, then he asked Dale where they should go to lay low. Before she could answer, Teddy got a call from a number he didn't recognize.

"My name is Sheldon Jeffrey, and I'm the United States secretary of commerce."

"How did you get this number?"

"I'm close to CIA Director Lance Cabot and he suggested we call you to alleviate our concerns about a problem with their representative in Macau."

"I appreciate your service to the United States, Mr. Secretary, but Lance Cabot is mistaken. Don't call this number again."

Teddy hung up and called Millie Martindale.

"Why is Lance Cabot giving out my number to people who don't trust you to do your job?"

"What are you talking about?"

Teddy told her about the call he'd just received and had to actually hold the phone away from his ear because Millie was yelling and cursing so loudly on the other end.

"I know who exactly is behind this," Millie said. "And maybe I'm tipping my hand at how much I know about you, but it would be great if the guy you were before you were Billy Barnett were to take care of this problem."

"That man is tired and wants to go back to L.A. and have pancakes for supper and sit on his deck facing the beach, listening to the ocean."

"I don't like the sound of that guy at all."

"Well, the guy you're talking to now needs a safe house in Macau."

"You know, I think there might be a way for both of us to help each other out and get back at this jerk at the same time."

"I'm listening," Teddy said.

"I'm here with a delegation of representatives from the U.S. government to help facilitate the testimony of a key Chinese witness."

"Li Feng," Teddy said.

"Maybe we should all get together then, my delegation of government officials, you, and your team in Macau."

"I don't work with a team."

"I also know you don't need a safe house in Macau for

yourself. So you're obviously working with someone while you're here."

"I don't think she would have any interest in sitting around a table with a bunch of old white men making casually racist Asian jokes at her expense."

"Suit yourself. I'll send you the address to a place I've been myself, so I know it's in tip-top shape."

"How do I know you haven't set any traps there for me?" Teddy said.

"We'll meet the rest of my gang at an American-themed diner near the airport."

◆ ◆ ◆

Rick's Café couldn't have been any more of a clichéd American tourist trap if it tried, and the delegation from the U.S. government was wallowing in it. Millie had sent Teddy the coordinates to a safe house where he left Dale Gai before heading to meet with Millie and her circus of politicians and career government cronies. They were all already seated in a booth at the back of the restaurant when Teddy arrived. Millie was sitting at the end of the booth closest to Teddy. She looked like a stranger who'd sat down with the group and didn't belong at all.

"I don't trust Arrow Donaldson and I think he's trying to intentionally keep Li Feng away from me, away from us, and it's not because he believes he can provide her better security."

"Then why don't we cut him out?" Secretary Jeffrey asked. "We have that power, right? We can get Li Feng ourselves and take her over to Hong Kong ourselves, right?"

"In theory, yes, Mr. Secretary," Millie said. "But in reality, we still don't know where Li Feng *is* and I think that's Arrow's goal. Keep playing hide-and-seek with her, sending us all over Macau looking for her or any other decoys he's stashed around town, until it's time for her testimony. Then he shows up before we can cut him out."

"Why are we meeting with a movie producer about such a high-profile mission?" Secretary Jeffrey asked.

"You of all people at this table should already know the answer to that question, since you somehow got Lance Cabot to give you my private cell phone number," Teddy said.

Jeffrey's face went white as the other men at the table looked at him suspiciously.

"Ms. Martindale has brought me in to use my connection to the film festival and to a side project it seems Mr. Donaldson is working on with the witness. I have a good chance to find out where she is before he can move her or hide her again," Teddy said.

49

LI FENG THOUGHT SHE FOUND HER MOMENT TO STRIKE Sonny Ma when she saw him leaving the hotel. She watched as he managed to bypass the throngs of fans and media, but then she lost him. She'd escaped her security detail enough growing up though to put herself in Sonny Ma's mind-set and think about where he might be. A few blocks later she spotted him again in a back alley. He didn't seem as aware of his surroundings as she would have expected him to be, but she stayed well behind him just in case. Another few blocks later, Li Feng realized he hadn't just left the hotel for a quick meal or fresh air. He was heading toward his mother's house.

Sonny Ma's mother lived in a retirement complex called the 24 Diamonds, super-luxury villas a few blocks off the Cotai Strip. Security was tight at the complex, and each resident had access to a fleet of diamond-encrusted Rolls-Royces to drive them around, making entry on her own virtually impossible for Li Feng. Luckily, she had been friends growing up with the man who developed the property.

Ten minutes later, she was riding in one of the diamond-encrusted Rolls on her way to help set up a surprise birthday party for Mrs. Ma, or so she'd told her old friend. Inside the villa, she was greeted at the door by the largest man she'd ever seen in her life.

"I'm a family friend," Li Feng said. "I've come for a visit."

"Ma'am is resting now. I just gave her tea and pills."

So this man was a nurse as well as security. She suspected that was Sonny Ma's doing. All of this had been paid for with his money, the fortune he'd made in his tech business.

As she looked around the entryway of the villa, Sonny Ma appeared from a back room and joined his mother's nurse/guard. Li Feng froze.

"It's good to see you, Li Feng," he said. "Would you join us in the tearoom?"

She nodded in astonishment and followed him through the massive villa to what seemed to be the most ornate room in the house. The ceiling was all glass, and there were plants growing along the walls, as well as a beautiful tree right in the middle of the room. Li Feng felt like she was outside in a private garden. A servant entered with a tray of tea and egg tarts, and after serving the tea left as quietly as she'd come.

Sonny Ma and Li Feng were alone together for the first time in more than a decade.

"I see what you've become publicly," Sonny Ma said, "and wonder what could have been if we'd had different childhoods."

"Our childhoods were an illusion," Li Feng spat out. "You stole my destiny."

"You are a billionaire executive with power and prestige. All I could have offered you was a life of crime and desperation."

"A life that leads to a home like this is worth a little desperation. And it would have been a life of *my own*."

"You speak like a silly child, Li Feng. I would give all my money to trade for what you have."

"Yet *you* are a legend," she replied, bitterly. "And you control your own destiny."

"Can you truly be so naïve? Your father came to me, told me to keep you away from that life. He's a more powerful man than I could ever become and has the backing of the government! If I'd ignored him, he would have come after me, or my family. Your anger is not with me. Your anger is with your family. Your anger is with your country."

"I was naïve, it seems, to believe that you would never back down. That you would help me fight for the life I wanted."

With that, Li Feng turned on her heel and stormed out of the bungalow.

♦ ♦ ♦

Millie had just entered the lobby of the Golden Desert Casino when her cell phone rang. It was Quentin.

"The preliminary analysis came back on the drone that killed your decoy," he said. While the drone itself was still in transit to the lab, Quentin had been able to send the techs at Quantico the data he'd pulled from its hard drive.

"And?"

"From everything they could see, it has the signatures of a local gangster named Sonny Ma. They'll be able to get more off the physical wreckage, but this should be enough to give you some direction in your investigation until I get back."

"Thank you so much, Quentin. This is great."

"You know, they have labs in Macau that could have analyzed this in a timelier fashion," Quentin said.

"But I don't trust them as much as I trust you."

"I'm glad to hear it," Quentin said, laughing. "I've got to go. Have fun saving the world."

50

TEDDY HAD HIS FEET UP ON THE COFFEE TABLE IN STONE'S suite and was watching a game show from the 1980s when Millie Martindale came through the door. She poured herself a drink from the bar and sat down next to him.

"Gin and tonic?" Teddy asked.

She took a sip then nodded.

"I always hate those fancy clear decanters because you can't tell what's in them," she said. "Especially with the clear liquors. I was hoping for gin or vodka and not tequila, which always makes me sick."

Teddy stood up and went to the bar and grabbed the decanter Millie had used and brought it back to her.

"People rarely put tequila in decanters, even though it's one of the best liquors for it. If they do, though, it tends to be obvious with the word *tequila* etched into the glass or some kind of cactus decoration. With vodka it's usually thick glass to help keep it chilled and the stopper is always in very tight. With gin, most of the best brands have subtle golden or blue hues so they're served in decanters with absolutely clear magnifying glass to enhance those hues."

"They teach you that in spy school?" Millie asked.

"Believe it or not, that was part of my movie industry learning. Alcohol knowledge is very important in the entertainment industry. Stone and Peter Barrington gave me and Dino and Ben a private lesson a while ago that included a robust discussion of decanters and how not to end up drinking tequila when you want gin and how to get water into your glass without anyone noticing to keep yourself from getting too drunk when you need to stay at a party long enough to make a deal or get vital information."

"Who would have thought that the training for being a movie producer would be useful for a spy or vice versa?"

"I wasn't just pumping my own ego when I was telling those D.C. stuffed suits that the entertainment industry has invaded every nook and cranny of our country."

Teddy didn't realize until he saw the look on Millie's face that he had just let some major secrets of his loose. He suspected Millie knew most of it already if she'd been working with Lance Cabot, but confirmation of any part of his current or past activities was never something he volunteered. He'd been in Macau long enough and was well-rested enough that jet lag and exhaustion were no longer an excuse for his lax behavior regarding security, so maybe there was an underlying reason.

Back in L.A. he'd been working hard to establish his own identity separate from Stone Barrington and then from Peter and Ben. He'd won an Academy Award as Billy Barnett as part of the production team for his last film with Peter and as Mark Weldon, he'd also won for Best Supporting Actor.

Before he'd been dragged to Macau, he'd been scouting locations for a film he'd packaged himself and was hoping to star in as Mark Weldon without Peter or Ben's direct involvement. Dale Gai and Millie Martindale seemed like potential partners as he developed his own team.

"You look like I lost you," Millie said. "Were you deep in thought about decanter glass choices?"

"What can I help you with, Millie?"

"The FBI looked at data from the drone that killed Li Feng's decoy and they traced it back to a local gangster named Sonny Ma."

Teddy didn't like that she had more evidence linking Sonny Ma to this whole thing. Maybe Kevin had gotten it wrong and Sonny Ma really was trying to kill Li Feng and make it look like Arrow was responsible. Teddy didn't know why he would do that, and he'd seemed genuine enough about wanting to leave that part of his life behind, but Teddy could also seem genuine when he needed to, when his life depended on it and he'd seen plenty of criminals who really did want to leave but were unable to for any number of reasons.

"How did the FBI get that data so quickly?" Teddy asked.

"My . . . friend Quentin Phillips is a special agent with the FBI and he took the drone with him when he flew back to the U.S."

"The FBI was able to analyze the physical wreckage of the drone?"

That would be a huge advantage over just the electronic data which he'd given to Kevin the last time he'd seen Sonny Ma implicated in a related scheme.

"Well, not exactly. Not yet."

Teddy was already doing the math in his head about when the FBI's plane would have left Macau and when it would land.

"He's still in the air," Teddy said.

"He sent them the data from the drone over e-mail and they'll confirm it with the physical wreckage when he lands."

Teddy found a scrap of paper and a pen and wrote down an e-mail address he knew Kevin Cushman would have immediate access to.

"Have your friend e-mail everything he sent to the FBI to this address as well."

"'Warplord'?" Millie asked.

"We all have identities from earlier in our lives that we regret but can't change," Teddy said.

She emptied the rest of her drink and poured another before stepping into the bathroom. When she emerged a few minutes later, she nodded, and Teddy waited to hear from Kevin. A former priest from Philadelphia had just been whammied on *Press Your Luck* when Kevin called the suite's phone next to Teddy.

"This one is bogus, too," Kevin said.

"Bingo?"

"Bingo."

51

ARROW DONALDSON WAS HAVING HIS MORNING COFFEE and watching the sun rise over his construction site when he got word that the congressional delegation arrived in Hong Kong, and he called his car and driver immediately so he could head to the consulate to meet them. He didn't have nearly the influence within Hong Kong that he did in Macau, but because the two administrative regions worked together in many areas, Arrow realized early on that he needed some sort of connection on the other island. He'd meticulously cultivated a network of reliable sources that had just paid great dividends.

Arrow's driver dropped him at the VIP entrance of the consulate. Inside, Arrow found the group in an executive conference room, just outside of the secure conference room where Li Feng would give her testimony. They all looked disoriented and jet-lagged and Arrow wondered if he'd made a mistake seeing the group before they'd had a chance to rest and collect themselves. But he knew the CIA had him in their sights, and they might try to undermine his reputation with the delegation. Under the circumstances, time wasn't a luxury he had to waste.

"Welcome to the command center, gentlemen," Arrow said, closing and locking the door behind him. The delegates remained silent and avoided eye contact with him.

He sat down in an empty seat not at the head, but at the middle of the table, an exhibition of humility. He put on an inviting smile, and gestured to the other chairs. This seemed to ease the tension in the room. Though, as the delegates took their own seats, no one spoke.

"I'm glad to see you've all made it here," Arrow said. "I hope Ken Joo took care of you."

"Where is Li Feng?" Secretary Jeffrey asked.

"She's housed in a secure location—as you know, the Chinese government has no interest in allowing her to testify. In fact, for that reason I believe we should move up the testimony to tomorrow, or possibly tonight if we can confirm the room in time."

Jeffrey gave Arrow an even look. "We've been discussing this among ourselves," Jeffrey said, "and have decided to call off the testimony."

Arrow kept his gaze glued to the wall behind the

group as he processed the news. Only a small tic in his cheek could hint at his rage at his whole plan collapsing.

"You had this conversation without me or any other representatives on hand?"

Jeffrey said nothing.

"May I ask your reasoning?"

"Concerns were raised that—"

Arrow's eyes narrowed. "Raised by whom?"

"—that the testimony has put Li Feng in mortal danger. The attempt on her life made that clear."

Millie Martindale had clearly wasted no time catching the delegation's ear.

"And given that extraordinary attack," Jeffrey continued, "we feel it most prudent to cancel and return to American soil." Left unsaid, Arrow realized with contempt, was that the delegates feared being targeted themselves.

"So we just abandon all the good work we've done here and go home? Let China win because a bunch of old men got cold feet at a resort?"

"Mr. Donaldson, we're prepared to recommend to the president that the ban on QuiTel be instated effective immediately without risking Li Feng's safety to have her testify. The attempts on her life are evidence enough of the veracity of her claims."

At that, Arrow blinked. "That's great. Great for the country, and for Li Feng," he said.

"And great for your business interests as well," a younger guy next to Secretary Jeffrey said.

"That's enough, gentlemen," Jeffrey said, mostly to his colleague. He turned back to Arrow. "Ms. Martindale doesn't know about our decision yet. We thought she would be here with you and Li Feng. We'd like for her to hear this from us rather than from you."

"Of course," Arrow said. "I'll have Li Feng moved to the second-phase housing I've arranged for her, before she heads off on her new, protected life. Thank you for your help and your service to our country."

◆ ◆ ◆

Back in his car, Arrow's mind was racing. Without the testimony, Arrow worried Li Feng would flip on him. He was pretty sure that *planning* to lie to Congress wasn't a crime and that as long as she didn't go through with it, she was safe from prosecution. Arrow, on the other hand, would be a perfect candidate for obstruction of Congress at best, and conspiracy or treason if the right people decided he needed to be made an example.

It would be much easier if he could just tell Bingo to kill Li Feng, but that would look suspicious this soon. He didn't want to give the CIA or the FBI any reasons to look at him more closely. Arrow still had Li Feng's coveted new identity papers and was helping her orchestrate her revenge on Sonny Ma. That should be enough, but he also knew the CIA had the same sort of resources available if they decided to help her out in exchange for evidence against him. He needed to go to Li Feng and talk to her in person and remind her of his power, and what could happen if she betrayed him.

Arrow told his driver to take him to Li Feng. Even though his driver didn't say anything, Arrow noticed the man suddenly avoided eye contact and grew suspiciously quiet the rest of the drive to the bunker.

52

MILLIE WAS STILL THINKING ABOUT QUENTIN AND THE FAKE drone data from the FBI when she got off the ferry in Hong Kong. She didn't blame the FBI for coming to the wrong conclusion given the data they had, but she wondered about the future of their agencies if guys like Kevin Cushman in his basement could beat them to this kind of information. Maybe people like Kevin, and her friend with the many names, were the future of this work rather than the bloated bureaucracy it had become.

Her car dropped her off at the consulate and she made her way toward the secure conference room where Li Feng would be giving her testimony. She knew her congressional buddies had already arrived, and after leaning on a few contacts she'd made in Macau, she found out their entire itinerary from the hotel in Macau to the ferry, and then their lodging in Hong Kong across from the consulate. Originally assuming she'd find the gang at their hotel eating or drinking or gossiping, she'd found out they'd been dropped off at the consulate instead of the hotel.

Millie hated feeling like she was always playing catch-up with Arrow, but on reflection she realized it wasn't a bad thing. In fact, it was necessary—she was here to figure out his angle and catch him in wrongdoing. But it was a delicate balance. She didn't want to give him so much free rein that he crossed the point of no return and did something destructive that she could have prevented. She didn't think they were at that point yet, but all signs pointed to them being close. That's why she needed to talk to the congressional delegation as quickly as possible and defuse whatever time bomb of information Arrow had planted in their heads.

As she approached the secure conference room, she was disheartened to see the delegates exiting the executive conference room and heading as a group toward the exits. Whatever Arrow had told them seemed worse than she had anticipated.

Secretary Jeffrey stepped forward from the pack and put his arm around Millie to move her farther away from the group. She quickly shrugged out of the awkward and inappropriate touching and moved back toward the group. Jeffrey looked at her like a parent waiting for a young child to make a connection on their own, seeming disappointed rather than angry.

"Your work here has been commendable, Ms. Martindale, and we'll be certain to pass that along to anyone who needs to hear it. In fact, your work has been so thorough, we no longer need to be here. The testimony has been called off."

"You can't do that. Without the testimony then no one will know—"

"The exception for QuiTel will not be renewed. Their business in the U.S. is done. The attack on Li Feng and all of the other chaos around this testimony convinced us, and our bosses, that the Chinese government had a vested interest in preventing her testimony. She had to be telling the truth. We talked to the president and her national security adviser, and they were in agreement. This is all because of you."

"No," Millie said. "This is because of Arrow Donaldson. He's the one who killed the decoy. He's the one who's behind the chaos around the testimony. Where's Li Feng now?"

Secretary Jeffrey looked confused.

"The last we heard from the FBI was that a former gangster named Sonny Ma is behind the chaos as he's been trying to reclaim his former criminal empire. He killed Arrow's decoy, thinking it was the real Li Feng. He may try again if we go through with the testimony. They grew up together and he's afraid her testimony to our government with expose his secrets. Her family is also very powerful, and some of our colleagues in the administration worry about looking like we're taking sides in a family dispute. We're better off getting out now and letting them fight amongst themselves."

"That's just what you're supposed to believe. A contact of mine who has done work for the Agency before in this capacity said the initial evidence made it look like Sonny Ma was responsible. But when he dug deeper into the data, he could see that Sonny Ma is being framed."

"Why should we believe this source of yours over our boys in the FBI?"

"He's the best there is," Millie said.

"It sounds like he's trying to be the smartest guy in the room by spreading conspiracy theories and lies. Why would anyone want to frame a gangster for crimes?"

"All the signs point to someone named Bing-Wen Jo, known as Bingo, and *he* works for Arrow Donaldson."

"If you ask me," Secretary Jeffrey said, "it sounds like someone is trying to frame Arrow Donaldson. And it sounds like they found the perfect mouthpiece in you."

Millie kept her mouth shut so she didn't say anything else they could use against her. She counted internally to ten, and then said, "Can you at least tell me where Li Feng is?"

Jeffrey shook his head.

"Arrow said he was moving her to the second-phase security he'd arranged for her after the testimony. She's in perfectly capable hands."

Nothing Millie could say would convince the delegates that they'd probably just handed Li Feng over to her death. She needed to get in touch with Li Feng, and she knew who could help.

53

"THEY'RE GOING TO GET HER KILLED," MILLIE SAID ON THE other end of the line as Teddy waited for the elevator. He'd been on his way to meet with the festival organizers when he'd picked up the phone to find Millie in a panic.

"I know you see it that way, and I understand that," Teddy said, "because your job is to protect her. But I also know that the testimony being called off is likely going to send Li Feng further off the deep end in her manic vendetta against Sonny Ma."

"So what do we do? I can't let her stay with Arrow, but you're right—if I get her away from him, she's not going to just go away quietly."

"I'm on my way down to talk to Sonny Ma and the festival organizers right now. I'm still here to make sure that whoever tried to ruin Peter and Ben's reputations gets what's coming to them. And right now, that looks like Li Feng."

"Arrow is moving her to his second-phase secure location, likely in Hong Kong where she was going to testify. I think he wants to get her out of the prying eyes of Macau. He's not as powerful over in Hong Kong, though, and I have contacts who can give me an idea of where he'd stash her. I'm going to see if I can convince her to get out of town before Arrow gets to her and maybe show her that her own life is more important than whatever need for revenge she has against a man."

Teddy sighed and wished once again he could get back to L.A., sit quietly on the beach, and stare at budgets and casting memos and insurance riders, all of the mundane behind-the-scenes details producers dealt with every day that he had taken for granted. But he stood outside the door of the suite thinking about what Millie said, and thinking about his own endgame.

All signs suggested Li Feng was behind the fake videos and blackmail of Peter and Ben as part of her larger play against Sonny Ma. Peter and Ben just happened to be at the wrong place at the wrong time. But he also knew that Li Feng had been harboring a grudge against Sonny Ma for decades, and it was only Arrow Donaldson who had been dumb enough or selfish enough to give her the resources to enact her revenge. And it was Arrow's men who had made the actual videos. Without Arrow's scheme to have Li Feng testify in the first place, none of this would ever have happened.

Teddy reached the door to the conference room housing the film festival organizers, and walked in. When all eyes turned to him, he said, "I think we should call the whole thing off."

Sonny Ma nodded as Teddy spoke.

"I was thinking the same thing. I have no desire for fame. I only agreed to this film because I thought it would lend legitimacy to the expansion of my business into casino technology. But it's done the opposite."

"It sounds like we're in agreement then," Teddy said.

The others in the room didn't look like they were in agreement on anything. They murmured and sighed and grumbled and finally one of them said, "Canceling isn't really an option. We would lose all of our money, and the film business in Macau would be even more tainted than it is now. We would never recover."

Unfortunately, Teddy knew they were right. And the festival had partnered with Centurion, and with Peter and Ben. He couldn't walk away and leave them in such dire straits.

He paced across the room, then back, thinking.

"Then maybe we should be the ones to kill Sonny Ma," Teddy said.

A collective gasp rose up, and Teddy would have smiled if the situation weren't so serious. Only Sonny Ma himself was oddly tranquil, seeing where Teddy was going.

"I don't believe our American friend is suggesting an actual murder," Sonny Ma said, looking toward Teddy. "I hope. I believe he is suggesting we do what we all do best: play make-believe."

"We can stage a publicity stunt, a fake assassination,

playing off Sonny Ma's reputation. After it's revealed that he wasn't really killed, he can talk about how the thought of being murdered was always at the back of his mind when he was involved with crime, and that's why he's determined to continue going legitimate."

The spokesman for the organizers looked back to the group, who seemed to be recovering from their shock.

"Much is at stake," the young man in the yellow suit said. "This is not just fun and entertainment. This is the image of the party. The image of China is at stake."

Teddy nodded and resisted the urge to stroke the sides of his head in contemplation. They were right again, and as an outsider, Teddy was never going to be able to answer those concerns. But he knew who could help.

"Let me discuss this with Dale Gai. We'll return when we have fully formulated a plan."

"Yes. Dale Gai. Good. This is good."

Sonny Ma didn't seem as confident, so Teddy waved him over to a private corner of the room.

"I realize this is not ideal for you," Teddy said, "but it's the one chance we have of taking care of a number of problems all at once. Li Feng will not go away and provide the U.S. government the evidence it needs to convict Arrow Donaldson until she sees you dead. With Li Feng gone, and Arrow Donaldson back in the U.S. facing criminal charges, your path to success with your online casino empire will be free and clear."

"Arrow's operation has been a frustrating irritant to my business."

"I'll control as much of this as I can. I'll fit you with

a protective vest padded with blood squibs that I'll explode by remote. I will direct Li Feng's effort to find a hitman toward me in disguise so that we don't risk someone else trying to kill you."

"I had no idea of the level of Li Feng's hatred of me until she came to my mother's house yesterday and went mad."

"Wait, Li Feng came to visit you? Was she with Arrow Donaldson?"

"She was alone."

Teddy processed that new information.

"Dale Gai and I will protect you, and at the end of this you'll be set up well for success. And I'll have all the pieces in place to punish those who smeared the good name of my friends."

Teddy left Sonny to find Dale. On the way he called Millie Martindale.

"Li Feng escaped from Arrow somehow, and visited Sonny Ma."

Teddy heard a muffled string of curse words and then, "Thank you," before Millie quickly hung up.

54

ARROW KNEW SOMETHING WAS WRONG THE MOMENT HIS driver pulled up to the safe house. Everything looked in order from the outside, but Arrow's driver had been skittish the entire drive.

"What happened?" Arrow asked when they arrived.

"Happened where? Here? Everything looks fine."

Arrow slammed his door shut and rushed inside the house. Li Feng was nowhere to be found. The driver was behind him in the doorway, and Arrow grabbed him by the front of his suit and threw him against the nearest wall.

"Where is she?"

"I don't know."

Arrow punched him in the chest and in the gut.

"What did you do with her?"

The driver was curled on the ground crying, muffling his words.

"She beat me," he said.

"She attacked you, so you let her go?"

The driver nodded his head.

"She said she would only be gone for a few minutes. She just wanted to get some fresh air."

Arrow kept his rage in check. Killing this man would be hard to clean up, and would get Arrow no closer to finding Li Feng. He went into the kitchen, grabbed a towel, and threw it to the driver on the floor.

"Did she say where she was going?"

"No, but she gave me her cell phone number so I could get ahold of her if I needed her."

Arrow had no doubt the number Li Feng had given this man was a fake, but he tried it anyway.

"It's disconnected. She gave you a fake number."

The driver coughed and took a deep breath before talking.

"I'm not an idiot. I checked first. It's a secure phone that can't be traced or receive calls. But you can send texts."

"Send her one. Tell her to come back."

While the driver sent a text message, Arrow called Bingo as a backup.

"Li Feng escaped," Arrow said. "Find her and bring her to the bunker. Alive."

"That lunatic is going to kill her," the driver said, struggling to stand up.

"He'll do what I tell him to do."

"He blames her for his family getting sent to the camps. He wants her dead, and you just let him know she's out from under your protection."

"Just because you are not loyal to me doesn't mean others are disloyal as well."

Arrow had thought the same thing about Bingo, but Li Feng's death would put a target on Bingo as much as it would on Arrow. When the heat blew over on all of this, Arrow would reward Bingo appropriately and all would be forgiven.

55

TEDDY WAS PLEASED TO FIND DALE QAI STILL AT THE SAFE house where he'd left her. He was less worried that the police would have tracked her to the off-the-books cabin and more worried that she might have left on her own, deciding she didn't need Teddy's help.

Dale was having tea and reading a book. She looked more relaxed than Teddy had seen her in their short time together. If he'd been a different person, he might have felt bad for dragging her back into the mess he was in. He sat down and had water instead of tea and gave Dale a brief summary of his meeting with Sonny Ma and the film festival organizers. When he was done, she was smiling mischievously.

"So, it seems the men in Macau continue to fail miserably," she said.

"A harsh judgment, but not wrong," Teddy said, somewhat abashed.

"And now you expect the women to come in and fix everything?"

"Not all the women, no, just one. You."

"What about your friend from the CIA?"

"How do you know about her?"

"Such a silly question to ask," Dale said. "It makes me wonder if you are as smart as I once thought you might be."

"I've been mistaken for a lot of things over the years, but smart isn't usually one of them."

Dale Gai cocked her head to the side and sipped on her tea. Teddy suspected she was trying to figure out what to make of him, and how much of herself and her life in Macau to risk to help him.

"Do you know Sonny Ma?"

"We are acquainted," Dale said

"Does that mean you'll help me fake his death in front of an audience?" Teddy asked.

Teddy remained silent while Dale contemplated her options.

"You need this to wrap everything up, don't you?"

"We all benefit, yes. Including you if Li Feng agrees to testify against Arrow Donaldson to the U.S. government and they send him away."

"I don't need this as much as you, but I would be in a better place with Sonny Ma owing me a favor. I'm in."

"Li Feng is not likely to try and kill Sonny Ma herself," Teddy said. "She had the perfect opportunity when she was alone with him at his mother's house."

"With her influence and family connections, there was no shortage of people she could have chosen from to carry out the job. But she can't use those connections now."

"That leaves hiring someone through the street scene grapevine. We should start at the pawnshop by Arrow's casino where Bingo followed me."

"Lunch first, then the pawnshop," Dale said.

◆ ◆ ◆

Lunch was pork chop bun sandwiches with iced lemon tea at a shop that looked like someone had opened a bodega in an abandoned maintenance shed. The pork chop bun was one of the greasiest and most delicious things Teddy had ever tasted.

When they arrived at the pawnshop, Teddy noticed the conversation was easier and less hostile than the last time he was there. Looking back on that interaction in hindsight, Teddy also suspected someone, probably Bingo, had been in the back room watching their interaction, which had probably been a source of stress for the man behind the counter.

Teddy wrote down an untraceable phone number that forwarded calls to the phone in his pocket. He slipped it across the desk, on top of a few large bills. "If Li Feng comes to you asking for someone to be a killer, you give her this number. That's all. You know Li Feng?"

The man nodded. Teddy waited for him to glance back toward the room behind him, maybe indicating that someone was watching, but the man kept his eyes on Teddy and Dale as he took the paper and the money, and discreetly placed them in his pocket.

56

MILLIE KNEW EXACTLY WHERE LI FENG WOULD BE GOING. Without the ability to draw on her family name and connections, she would need to consult the criminal underground. The only criminal underground she suspected Li Feng knew about would be the pawnshop near the casino. And since Li Feng wouldn't want to risk being seen by anyone, she'd keep her travels to alleys and the more out-of-the-way paths.

The cab dropped Millie off at the pawnshop, and she worked her way back toward the safe house, hoping to catch Li Feng off guard. Her plan paid off. Several blocks later, Millie spotted her quarry coming out of a restaurant. Millie sped up her pace.

◆ ◆ ◆

The sting of seeing Sonny Ma and his pathetic dismissal of her anger at him was still raging inside Li Feng as she made her way through the darker and more anonymous parts of Macau.

Ziggy Peng had been right to question her elaborate plan that she could now admit was also silly. As she wandered the streets, her anger increasing rather than dissipating, she thought about killing Sonny Ma. Ziggy Peng had been dismissive of her and had whined about every aspect of her plan. She had no more patience for pathetic men to do her bidding for her. She would kill Sonny Ma herself.

She ducked into a small café to get something to eat. She expected that the combination of food and the clarity that she would be the one to kill Sonny Ma would put her at ease, but all it did was raise more questions in her mind. It was taking everything she had and all of her concentration to just stay in the shadows and not get recognized on the street. This was only reinforced in her mind when she stepped out of the café and back into the alley and was accosted by a street thug. It was a dirty kid who had an inch or so on her and was about twenty pounds heavier. He pressed her against the wall with his arm against her throat and his other hand over her mouth.

"Money, now. No mouth," the thug said.

She shook her head and tried to speak.

"I don't have any money," she mumbled through the thug's hand.

She heard a *click* and felt a prick against her neck as the thug held a switchblade to her throat. A second person appeared from the shadow, probably an accomplice. Li Feng was certain she was about to die.

"Saia daqui agora," the second person said in Portuguese. Li Feng knew that meant *Get out of here now.*

♦ ♦ ♦

"Saia daqui agora," Millie said, feeling more comfortable with her Portuguese than her Mandarin at the moment.

The thug dropped his arm from Li Feng and scrambled away.

Putting one hand over the small wound on her neck, Li Feng looked at her rescuer.

"My name is Millie Martindale. I'm with the CIA and I can help you."

"I don't need your help."

"You'd be dead right now if I wasn't following you."

"What do you want from me?"

"I was the one who was supposed to be protecting you when you testified before the U.S. government."

"Brilliant job. Thank you."

"Without your testimony, I'm worried that Arrow Donaldson sees you as a loose end. I can protect you. I can get you a new identity and get you out of this country if you testify on the record against Arrow Donaldson."

"I have business in Macau beyond Arrow Donaldson."

Millie reached into her back pocket and pulled out a pair of zip ties and held them up.

"I can arrest you now and you get nothing."

Li Feng also took a more upright stance and flicked her wrist to show that she was now holding the switchblade knife she'd taken from her attacker.

"Come and get me."

Millie raised her hands in surrender and backed away as Li Feng came away from the wall, knife first. Li Feng turned and backed down the alley, then finally turned and ran.

57

LI FENG MADE HER WAY BACK TO THE MAIN STREET WHERE she was less worried about being recognized than being murdered or arrested. If she couldn't even get up the nerve to take down a street thug, how was she going to kill Sonny Ma?

That didn't mean she had to go begging to Arrow Donaldson for help again. He saw her as a charity case, and was doing things for her because she was doing things for him. That was no position for a woman like Li Feng to be in, owing people favors. She would do what she'd been trained in her upbringing to do when she needed something done that she didn't have the skill for: hire someone to do it.

Though Sonny Ma had cut her potential criminal career short at the request of her parents, Li Feng still had knowledge of Macau's underworld workings, both through her job and through her own explorations online of the digital hubs of crime in Macau. She knew there was one place in the part of town she was in where she could find what she needed and she headed to the pawnshop near the Golden Desert Casino.

Many of the men who ran illicit businesses in Macau owed her family or her family's corporation money and she didn't want to do business with any of those people lest it turn out just like with Ziggy Peng and Arrow Donaldson. But she knew the man who ran the pawnshop by the Golden Desert Casino was as close to an honest and independent man as you could get in the criminal world. She couldn't remember his real name, but online everyone referred to him as Donny Pawn. She had no idea where the name came from, but it was easier to remember than the man's real name or the more complicated name of his business.

Even though Donny Pawn was the name everyone used for him online, it didn't seem like the sort of name the man would be comfortable with her using in front of him at his place of business. She steeled her memory to make sure she wouldn't accidentally say it. Once inside the shop, it didn't matter. Names were not necessary, and it only took a few minutes of seemingly banal small talk loaded with double meaning for her to walk out of the pawnshop with the phone number of a man who would take her money to kill Sonny Ma.

♦ ♦ ♦

Teddy motioned for Dale to sit next to him on a bench in front of Macau's replica of the Eiffel Tower when his phone rang. The call was being forwarded from the number they'd left with the pawnbroker. It had to be Li Feng.

"You've reached the man," Teddy said, quoting a line from a movie where he'd played a hitman in his Mark Weldon identity. Peter Barrington had written the script, and it seemed appropriate to use Peter's words to set this plan in motion.

"I have a man I wish to have you deal with," the woman said.

"Is this man important?"

"My money is what's important, and there's plenty of it for you to claim."

Teddy wanted to meet her in person to make sure that Li Feng was the one hiring him, and he wanted to meet somewhere that criminals would meet. The only place he could think of was the karaoke bar where they'd talked with Kwok Lin, which seemed shady enough for his purposes. He named an amount off of the top of his head, and instructed Li Feng to meet him at the bar with the cash in fifteen minutes.

"How do I know you won't steal it from me when we meet?"

"You don't," Teddy said. "If I do, you can hire someone else to kill me and get your money back."

58

THE KARAOKE BAR WAS NOT VERY FAR AWAY FROM THE casino. Teddy was about to head out after hanging up with Li Feng when he wondered if he should change his look. The average person wouldn't recognize Billy Barnett, but he'd heard repeatedly that she was a fan of American movies and wanted to be an actress. There was a real chance that she had been watching the Academy Awards last year when he was on stage as a winner, and again after an explosion rocked the broadcast.

That would be just his luck to come halfway around the world only to be identified from a TV broadcast. As he thought about that, he realized he'd been telling himself a lie. There was no relaxation on the beach waiting for him back in L.A. Trouble followed wherever he went. Or rather, there was trouble everywhere in the world, and he felt obligated to use his skills to help friends—and occasionally former enemies—when they ran into trouble.

The last time he had tried to go away and relax was after his wife, Betsy, had died. He'd driven out to Santa Fe to visit an old friend and ended up saving his friend's life as well as hunting down the man who killed Betsy.

And he enjoyed it. He could have quit and gone all in on Billy Barnett or Mark Weldon, but those were more than just fake names on fake paper. They were men with jobs and with family and friends and coworkers who didn't have Teddy's skills or Teddy's connections. Many men and several governments had tried to kill Teddy, and it seemed that even Teddy himself couldn't completely kill his original identity.

He looked around the suite for whatever was left of the production makeup he'd used for his disguises so far and wasn't happy with what he saw. There was a knock at the door, and Dale's face lit up with a giant smile that he hadn't suspected she was capable of.

"Oh, good. I have a surprise for you," she said.

"Is it the man you hired to kill me?"

"I'm not telling you when he arrives."

Teddy didn't laugh right away as a part of him believed she might only be partially kidding about that, but before he could think any longer about it, Dale had the door open and was waving in a man carrying into the suite what looked to be Teddy's luggage.

"You didn't," Teddy said, giving his own unexpected wide smile. "Is this all my luggage?"

"I completely forgot I'd contacted the airport to send it here until they called to let me know it arrived. Sergeant Lam says hello."

"I don't believe that at all. This is wonderful and the timing couldn't be better."

Teddy tipped the luggage man and excused himself to the bathroom to get into costume. The first look he tried seemed natural in his head, but both he and Dale could tell when he emerged that a white man like Teddy dressing as an Asian man was a terrible idea, even if no offense was intended. Teddy went back to the bathroom and came out the next time dressed like a Russian hitman he'd met once named Zosima.

◆ ◆ ◆

Without his driver and without Bingo by his side, Arrow Donaldson felt lost in Macau. He was one of the most important men in the city, but he might as well have been a tourist to those around him. Arrow viewed it as strong leadership to delegate so much to others in his organization, but he was realizing that he'd lost touch with the core of his business. His driver was waiting at the bunker for Li Feng to contact him, and Bingo was out doing his own search. But Arrow didn't want to sit behind a desk and wait for a phone call.

He'd taken his car and driven himself along the main strip and then circled around the outskirts before parking in the underground lot at the Hollywood City Casino. Walking around among the shoppers and gamblers and families, he felt lonely and depressed. This was no way to live a life. Even if these people put millions of dollars a year in his pocket through their desperate attempts at a weekend of happiness, he had no interest in being around them. He was eating a pretzel from a vendor at the heart of the mall adjacent to the casino when Bingo called. Arrow spit the pretzel into a trash bin and answered.

59

BINGO WAS CHASING HIS SOURCES AROUND TOWN, TRYING to keep track of Billy Barnett and Li Feng, when he got a call from the pawnbroker he'd been watching earlier.

"Li Feng is looking to hire a man to kill Sonny Ma. You were good to me when you were here last, and I am appreciative."

Bingo called Arrow with the news.

"This doesn't change anything," Arrow said. "Watch her. When Sonny Ma is dead, grab her."

♦ ♦ ♦

"I am Zosima," Teddy said when Li Feng sat down and handed him an envelope of money. Teddy flipped through it for appearance's sake but knew it would all be there.

"That is a wonderful made-up name," Li Feng said, archly. "Like the book, *The Brothers Karamazov.* You did not sound Russian when we spoke on the phone."

Teddy shrugged a shoulder and winked in acknowledgment of her cleverness. They both knew that what he called himself, or pretended to sound like, served as his protection and was none of her business.

"You know Sonny Ma?"

"I know many people. It does not matter if I know the man I am supposed to kill. You give me a name, I do the job."

"I don't merely want him killed," Li Feng said. "I want his death to be *spectacular.* A spectacle to be remembered, the only thing anybody will ever recall about him after his death."

"This envelope should be thicker for such a job. This was not mentioned on the phone."

"I'll get you whatever money you need."

She handed Teddy a flyer for the movie's premiere during the film festival.

"This is where Sonny Ma must die."

Teddy pretended to examine the flyer, though he already knew the contents by heart. "I will do this job at this premiere, and you will pay me extra when it's done."

"How will you make sure I pay? You don't know who I am."

"You will pay or you will die."

"I hope your skills as a hitman are better than your lines. You sound ridiculous."

She was laughing, but Teddy leaned in closer so he could make sure she heard every word, even with the loud bar noise around them.

"You will pay," he said, slowly, in his regular voice. "Or you will die."

60

WHEN TEDDY AND DALE WERE SURE THAT LI FENG WAS gone, they left their table at the karaoke bar and went outside where they checked again to make sure Li Feng wasn't hanging around to try and follow them. Teddy thought Dale was being overly paranoid, but she knew this area and the people better than Teddy, so he deferred to her expertise. While Teddy was agreeing with her, Dale motioned for a passing car to stop for them. It was a private car, not a taxi.

"You already arranged this, didn't you?" Teddy asked.

She shrugged and got into the back seat of the car. Teddy hated sitting in the front seat for security and personality reasons, so he squeezed into the small back seat next to Dale. Their legs were touching and as they shifted into positions as comfortable as they were able to find, their pants legs shimmied up and there was a moment where they were touching each other ankle to ankle and skin to skin and Teddy felt an electric burst in his chest.

He could tell Dale felt it, too, and he simultaneously wanted to sink further into the seat and get closer to her while also jumping out of the car and getting as far away from her as possible. This certainly wasn't the first time Teddy had gone from suspicion to fireworks with a woman, but it was the first time since his wife that it felt that way.

Dale was still making small talk with the driver when they arrived at Macau Tower. Teddy was grateful she didn't seem to care that he was oblivious to the conversation. The Tower was striking in its height and gloss. It didn't have the old-world charm of some of the other buildings, but it wasn't as garish as the casino towers and the newer additions to the skyline. The concrete tower was topped with a glistening orb of chrome and emerald green glass that looked like the prime jewel on top of a massive scepter.

"The cinema has three screens. The premiere will be held at the top of the Tower, on the largest movie screen in all of China," Dale said, when it seemed like she was certain Teddy was actually listening again.

Dale led the way from the car through the small luxury shopping center at the base of the Tower and then up the elevator to the top of the Tower. Each step, and each new aspect of the environment Teddy saw made him more and more nervous about how he would be able to pull this off. He never doubted that he would be able to make it work, and having someone of Dale Gai's skill and passion working with him made him even more certain. But the margin of error was going to be even slimmer than it normally was and the price of failure would be even more catastrophic than normal.

If this went sideways, not only would Teddy and Dale both likely die but also the relationship between the United States and China would explode. The best-case scenario under those circumstances would be a return to another Cold War. Worst-case scenario was another world war.

"Did you see the glass bridge and the bungee jumping setup?" Dale asked as Teddy looked around.

"I don't like anything about this," Teddy said.

"The fates wouldn't bring the two of us together for any ordinary fake murder-for-hire plot, now would they?" she said with a wry smile. "Two people like us require an exceptional intervention."

"The exceptional part will be if we manage to get out of this alive."

61

AS SHE LEFT THE KARAOKE BAR AFTER PAYING THE HITMAN with the ridiculous Russian name to kill Sonny Ma, Li Feng was regretting her choice to hire out the death of Sonny Ma. As she wandered the street, thinking back to her assault and wishing she would have been more aggressive, Li Feng decided she would keep the ridiculous Russian hitman as a backup. But this was a mission she wanted to do herself.

Li Feng went back to the pawnshop, since the owner there had already seen her. She wanted to keep her footprint in the area as small as possible until Sonny Ma was dead. Her plan was to buy a small pistol, but when she entered the store, the man behind the counter was polishing a small ornate sword. The only swords Li Feng had ever seen had been gaudy and impractical, like the ones Sonny Ma favored in his movies and as decoration in his offices. But this sword was small, slightly larger than a large kitchen knife, and had a plush red leather case and glittering bloodred hilt. This was going to be the weapon she used to kill the man who killed her dreams.

She gave the man her only remaining credit card, hoping it would still work, then walked out of the pawnshop with her new weapon. With the sword in her hand, she felt powerful, vindicated in her entire endeavor. There would be any number of guests at the event wearing swords to dress like Sonny Ma, so she didn't worry much about it being confiscated. She looked at her phone and the text from Arrow's driver that she'd been ignoring, and sent him a message back.

> Bring the nicest car you have access to, and an outfit appropriate for the film premiere.

She gave him a list of boutiques in the area that had her measurements and preferences on file, then hung up.

♦ ♦ ♦

Arrow left Hollywood City Casino in a foul mood and sat in his car outside of the bunker contemplating his next move. He hadn't contemplated much when his driver called.

"She just got back to me. Wants me to go get a dress for her and then pick her up for the premiere," he said.

This perked Arrow up greatly. He'd been stewing over the driver's comments about Bingo wanting to kill Li Feng. If he could find her out in a public place where she felt at ease, it might be easier to convince her to return to his protection.

"I'm out front with the car," Arrow said. "Tell her you're on your way."

While he waited for the driver, Arrow called Bingo.

"I don't need you on Li Feng anymore. I've got it covered. Meet me back at my suite and I'll take care of you."

◆ ◆ ◆

When Dale was finished with the tour of the Macau Tower complex, she and Teddy found Sonny Ma in the film festival's green room that looked out over the bungee jumping deck and the city below. It was a magnificent vista. Teddy rolled out all the luggage he'd brought from the hotel, and along with the extensive makeup and visual effects kits, he had a bulletproof Kevlar vest that he'd fitted with blood squibs. It was one of his own many inventions when he needed something that wasn't commercially available.

As Dale fit Sonny with the vest, Teddy hooked up the blood splatter mechanisms and explained to Sonny what exactly was going to happen. During the premiere, when Sonny Ma was introduced and brought to the front of the theater, Teddy would stand up and shoot him. The gun would be loaded with blanks, but while pulling the trigger Teddy would also activate the blood squibs. The resulting explosion of blood would make it appear that Sonny was really shot.

Before they could finish the briefing, they heard chatter from the others in the room that Li Feng had arrived in the lobby.

62

AFTER HER RUN-IN WITH LI FENG, MILLIE WAS MORE CAU-tious with her surveillance. It didn't matter where Li Feng was right then: Millie knew she would be at the movie premiere that evening. Millie's first idea was to gather the U.S. delegates and put them on a bus to the movie premiere so they could grab Li Feng and have her tell them everything she knew about Arrow's plans and what he had asked her to do. Millie had a lot of circumstantial evidence gathered from her sources in Macau and within Arrow's operation, but the last piece she needed was Li Feng, on the record, saying that Arrow was bribing her to lie to Congress about her family's company.

That plan hadn't worked because no one was taking her calls anymore now that the testimony was off. She wasted too much precious time trying to pull that together, and now her only option was to go to the premiere herself and try to talk to Li Feng one more time.

♦ ♦ ♦

The car that picked Li Feng up was not as fancy as she'd hoped, but she got in anyway and heard the *thunk* of the locks before she noticed Arrow sitting in the front passenger seat. She tried to escape, but the door wouldn't budge.

"We're here to keep you safe," Arrow said. "And we brought you a new dress."

Arrow handed her the dress they'd picked up from the boutique back to her.

"You can change in the car. We won't look."

She hesitated, but as the car pulled away from the pawnshop, she started undressing.

"What are you going to do to me?"

"What I promised. You'll get to see Sonny Ma killed, and then we'll escort you to the airport with your new identity and send you off on your new future in the U.S."

"Really?" She remained unconvinced.

"If I wanted you dead, you'd be in the trunk of this car instead of the back seat," Arrow said.

63

THE MACAU TOWER SHOPPING CENTER HAD A GLOSSY, high-end look most of the time, but the glass and chrome and marble had been covered with velvet and jewels and gold for this event. Li Feng strode into the lobby with a confident swagger, her dress clinging tightly to her body and her sword swaying with her hips. She saw Sonny Ma across the room and went to him as if she were his co-guest of honor.

The look on his face as she approached him was almost worth the effort itself. His eyes flickered back and forth looking for an exit, but she remained calm and tried to project an image of professionalism and not of crazy murder. For her to have the best shot of being as close as possible to this man when he died, she needed to charm him and stay close to him early on, even if the sickness in her stomach from it became unbearable. He seemed uncomfortable as well but wasn't backing away.

"I apologize for my behavior the last time we saw each other," she said, putting her hand on his arm as she spoke.

He flinched, but then quickly relaxed his arm instead of pulling it away when he realized she wasn't trying to grab him.

"We hadn't seen each other in many years," Sonny Ma said. "It was never going to be easy."

She tried to calm her burning anger so that she didn't waste her opportunity to give Sonny Ma his proper comeuppance. If she was ever going to be an actress, she was going to need to have precise control of her emotions. Her role this evening demanded her to be conciliatory, and she would play the role brilliantly.

"The world is changing, and I see you changing; I thought that maybe I could change, too."

She saw a spark in Sonny Ma's eyes and a flicker of a smile as she spoke.

"You still can. This new enterprise can be a fresh start for both of us. You could come work for me and help me build this new face of gambling in Macau."

The acid burned in her stomach as Li Feng choked back a biting response to Sonny Ma's insulting offer. She had no interest in being stuck in cubicles and boardrooms, or worse, being a trophy for Sonny Ma to parade around at boring functions.

Li Feng noticed the crowd that had been spread across the entire complex was now quickly collapsing in on them as everyone realized that Sonny Ma was in the room. Some even seemed to recognize Li Feng. She played her role well and was receiving the sort of attention she craved. It felt as good as she could have ever dreamed it would feel. It felt wonderful, but she needed to move him up to the area for the premiere so she could remain close to Sonny.

"Won't you escort me up to the premiere?" she asked.

He agreed, even though he still seemed skeptical. The entire way, she kept expecting someone to stop them and confiscate her sword. But she was lucky that so many festival attendees were wearing costumes with fake weaponry of their own. Alongside the others, hers didn't look out of place, and nobody bothered her about it.

◆ ◆ ◆

Bingo hung up with Arrow Donaldson and smashed his phone. He was not going to back off of Li Feng. She would have Sonny Ma killed, laugh at the man's demise, and then be rewarded with a new identity for success in the United States. He would keep to his plan and go to Macau Tower and kill Li Feng.

The Tower still took his breath away every time he saw it, but this time it was even more breathtaking because it would make it very difficult to keep an eye on Li Feng. Bingo saw Sonny Ma first because the giant man dominated any room he was in, but he was startled to see Li

Feng there with Sonny Ma, and holding a sword. Was this it? Was she going to kill him herself? The window disappeared as quickly as it had opened as the crowd noticed the two of them and quickly swarmed the pair, making it impossible for Bingo to make a move.

64

BACK IN THE GREEN ROOM, TEDDY FOUND DALE BRIEFING part of the security team on what was about to happen. Teddy listened as she commanded the conversation and conveyed the danger and process of their plan without divulging details that could compromise anyone involved. When she was done and everyone went out to their stations, Teddy approached her.

"It sounds like everything up here is wrapped up as much as possible," he said, "which is good because Li Feng just arrived carrying a sword."

"There's a whole sea of people down there wearing swords," Dale said. "It's Sonny Ma's trademark."

"I figured there would be plenty of fake swords, but I didn't think Li Feng was the sword type."

"She's currently chatting with Sonny Ma—peaceably,

it seems—who, it seems, will be escorting her to her seat at the premiere."

"That's . . . interesting."

"And right before I came up here, I saw Bingo arrive as well. It's a fifty-fifty guess whether he's here as Li Feng's backup hitman, or on a mission to kill *her*. The plan will still work if Bingo shoots Sonny Ma instead of you, correct?"

"Yes. My way is safer, because my gun is loaded with blanks, but as long as Bingo doesn't shoot him in the head it should be fine."

"What if Li Feng uses her sword?"

"Same thing, as long as she doesn't go for the head."

"It sounds like we should rethink security around Sonny Ma's head," Dale said.

"I'll talk to security and make sure they keep an eye on Bingo," Teddy said. "They need to lure him in but stop him before he tries to kill anyone."

♦ ♦ ♦

Li Feng reveled in the attention as she made her way through the lower level of the shopping and cinema complex with Sonny Ma. Though she knew most eyes were on the man the premiere was honoring, it was only a matter of time before she stole the spotlight.

When they reached the top floor and the premiere auditorium, she saw Sonny Ma gesture subtly to the ushers that his guest required a seat with him. The crew deftly made the necessary adjustments, and the couple sat down.

"The attention is intoxicating," Li Feng said. "How can you not crave this every day?"

"The kind of attention I used to attract was more dangerous than this. People used to try and kill me if they had my attention. I think the odds of someone trying to kill me at a gala like this are much smaller."

"Don't you worry with all of the swords around?"

"They're all play swords, I suspect. But these people all love me here."

"We've both had servants and staff to wait on us, but this feels different," Li Feng said. "Like they're making our lives easier because they love us and respect us, not because they're family servants or spies."

"I've grown fond of taking care of myself. I like doing things around the house for my mother and I like working in the garden in my building. Could you ever have imagined me gardening?"

They both laughed and Li Feng felt at ease for the first time all night.

"You should join *me*," Li Feng said. "We could be the power couple of the Chinese entertainment scene. We could even go over to the U.S."

The goodwill and wavering commitment that had been building through the conversation died right there as Sonny Ma went silent and turned away from her. Li Feng refused to return to a life behind a desk. It seemed Sonny Ma could not help her after all.

As the ceremony began, Li Feng looked around to avoid having to look at Sonny. She saw Arrow's right-hand man, Bing-Wen Jo, and then spotted the hitman who called himself Zosima. Were they both here to kill Sonny Ma? She was feeling better about her chances. Maybe they would all kill each other, and she could truly be free and in the clear.

When her attention came back around to Sonny Ma, she noticed he was standing and holding his hand out for her.

"Join me on stage. This talk has been wonderful and has made me appreciate where I'm from and where I'm going. Enjoy the spotlight you so desperately crave."

She didn't know why he was doing this, and the tone in his voice was more ominous than collegial. But with two men in the audience likely there to kill him, she wouldn't have to see to the deed herself, and if she was on stage when it happened she would seem like the least likely suspect. She might even be able to harness the attention to give her a boost in her new career.

Li Feng unhooked the sword from its sash around her waist and left it on her seat, then she joined Sonny Ma on stage.

65

BINGO DID NOT EXPECT SONNY MA TO BRING LI FENG UP onto the stage. He'd found a seat a few rows back from the stage, and from there he could see Dale Gai in the second row with some of the uniformed security personnel. She was talking to a garish man who looked like one of the Russian gangsters that had been coming to Macau lately looking to stir up interest in their own budding gambling city of Artem. Could Arrow Donaldson be looking to expand his own empire to Russia? Is that what Dale Gai had been involved in?

His curiosity about the mystery Russian man was squashed when he saw Li Feng on stage next to Sonny Ma. The lights shone bright on her, and the same rage and depression he'd experienced looking through the screen on his drone when he killed her decoy came rushing back. This was his chance to make it all right. He would kill Li Feng. He would kill Sonny Ma.

Bingo reached down to the gun clipped to the back of his pants and slipped it out. Two of the security guards on the edge of the auditorium seemed to notice him and one of them moved slightly toward Bingo, but no one tried to stop him as he approached the second row and Dale Gai.

♦ ♦ ♦

Teddy was surprised when Li Feng joined Sonny Ma on stage, but it didn't change the plan. In fact, Teddy was quite pleased because he would have easy access to detain Li Feng after the shooting without having to hunt her down. Teddy made sure the gun in his hand was ready, and he stood to fire.

♦ ♦ ♦

As Bingo reached Dale Gai's row, he noticed two things. First, he saw the sword Li Feng had been carrying was lying on the seat she'd vacated. The second thing he noticed was that the mystery Russian man sitting next to Dale was about to shoot Sonny Ma.

The Russian fired three times and Sonny Ma's chest exploded. In the chaos that erupted, Bingo put his gun away and grabbed the sword so he could chop Li Feng's head off like the demon that she was.

♦ ♦ ♦

The blood from Sonny Ma's chest soaked Li Feng, and she was delighted. This was the role she was meant to play, the grieving old friend. She wailed as Sonny's body fell on top of hers, her dress ripping on the way down. She couldn't have choreographed the moment any better herself.

To most in the room, she'd appear as much a victim as Sonny Ma. She could not imagine a more perfect ending to her plan. Sonny Ma murdered in front of his fans, and she would be fawned over as a witness and a grieving friend rather than investigated as a suspect. There would be talk-show appearances and interviews and photo shoots.

While Sonny fell to the ground and her Russian hitman looked to escape, Li Feng noticed Bingo charging the stage with her sword. Sonny Ma was already dead. She smiled again at that thought, and only when it was too late did she realize why Bingo was coming toward the stage.

Arrow Donaldson had lied to her. He wasn't going to keep his end of the deal. He wanted her dead.

♦ ♦ ♦

After shooting Sonny Ma, Teddy thought his part was over. When he saw Bingo pass him in the aisle of the theater then grab the sword Li Feng left behind, Teddy knew he still had more work to do. With Sonny Ma apparently dead, the only other target Teddy saw on stage was Li Feng. Teddy hoped to get to the stage before Bingo, but he wasn't going to make it in time.

Teddy was about to scream for Li Feng to move. Then at the last second, Sonny Ma stood up and dived in front of the sword. He collapsed back to the ground, and Teddy had to decide which villain he was going to try and capture.

66

THE CROWD IN THE MOVIE THEATER PANICKED AND PEOPLE were pushing toward the exits, but the security personnel was doing an admirable job of keeping everyone as calm and orderly as possible. Teddy decided to pursue Bingo rather than Li Feng, but he wasn't going to be able to do much with a gun loaded with blanks. Bingo had been stunned briefly after the impact of his sword hitting the Kevlar vest on Sonny Ma, but he was getting back to his feet. Once again, Teddy found himself without a viable weapon when he needed one. He tossed the gun to the ground and looked to see if Dale Gai was able to help, but she was tending to Li Feng, who had been pushed off the stage during the commotion.

Bingo ran from the theater to the surrounding walkway where he ran smack into a crowd of screaming people.

Teddy was right behind him and in one swift motion, pulled his sport coat off and slung it around Bingo, stopping his movement temporarily.

"It's not too late to surrender," Teddy said. "I can protect you if you turn on Arrow Donaldson."

Bingo grunted and pulled his way out of Teddy's improvised straitjacket. He brought the sword back up to Teddy's face, but Bingo didn't seem as comfortable with the sword as Teddy thought he was and used that to his advantage. Teddy went after Bingo barehanded and was able to survive longer than most would against someone like Bingo, but he wasn't going to get far without a weapon.

Teddy struck Bingo in the throat with his hand and took advantage of Bingo's loss of breath to knee him in the groin. The sword dropped to the ground and Teddy picked it up. He wasn't comfortable with the weird weight, balance, and dull blade of the ornamental sword, either. Bingo scored a free shot to the side of Teddy's head that disoriented him. While Teddy crumpled to the floor, Bingo made a run for it.

While Teddy recovered from the cheap hit from Bingo, he noticed the police were making their way up to the top level. Teddy didn't have the time or the interest to deal with the police at that moment, so he slipped into the men's room and stripped off the Russian hitman clothes and revealed tacky tourist clothes underneath. He hadn't seen too many Russian tourists in Macau, but he'd seen enough to know he wouldn't stick out in the crowds.

The crowds were thick and angry, and Teddy easily blended in as the police passed them by. When he was able to extract himself from the crowd, he looked down over the glass bridge and saw that Bingo had made it to the bottom of the Tower and was exiting the lower-level shopping center. If Teddy couldn't catch up with him in the next several seconds, Bingo would likely disappear and Teddy's best chance at getting justice for Peter and Ben would be gone.

At the end of the glass bridge, Teddy saw the bungee jumping station Dale had shown him. He didn't have time to strap himself into the rig and then unstrap it when he got to the bottom, or wait for someone to unhook him if he didn't quite make it to the bottom, so he looked to the line of tandem jumpers.

One instructor was already strapped into a harness and connected to the cord and the tandem jumper was almost finished getting strapped into her harness. Teddy put himself in the mind-set of stuntman Mark Weldon and pushed his way to the front of the line.

"I apologize terribly for what I'm about to do," Teddy said, as he grabbed the instructor as tightly as he could and pushed them both off the jump deck.

Teddy pointed them as straight downward as possible so they had maximum speed. At the very bottom of the drop, just before they would snap and bounce back up toward the platform, Teddy spied the safety net he was aiming for and pushed himself off the plummeting jumper just as the cord snapped taut.

Teddy slammed into the edge of the safety net, taking

the landing more roughly than he'd hoped. He could still run, though, and Bingo was just about to pass when Teddy hopped off the safety net and landed on top of him. Bingo fought back, but Teddy quickly regained the upper hand and wrapped Bingo in a wrestling hold one of the stunt coordinators on his last movie had taught him.

"Tell me Arrow Donaldson was behind those videos of Peter and Ben."

Bingo struggled but didn't say anything.

"Or was it Li Feng?"

Teddy tightened his grip on Bingo, crushing the man's chest and putting immense pressure on his arms.

Bingo struggled to speak. "Li Feng would prostitute herself to your American friends, not ruin them. I put them in the video to make them pay. You American movie men think you can—"

Teddy was in no mood to listen to a long speech now that he had in his hands the main person responsible for setting up Peter and Ben. Teddy swung his feet out, caught Bingo's legs at the knees, and dropped him to the ground.

"I don't want to hear it," Teddy said. "But I don't want to kill you here on this hill unarmed unless I have to."

Teddy let go of Bingo and took a step back.

Bingo went for Teddy's throat.

"I will kill Li Feng, I will kill—"

Teddy sighed as he whipped his hand out and hit Bingo in the throat, then wrapped his arms around Bingo's neck again and snapped it.

67

TEDDY WENT BACK TO THE TOWER TO PIECE TOGETHER what else had happened while he'd been fighting Bingo. He arrived just in time to see Sonny Ma and the festival organizers giving a press conference about how they had used the skills and talents of the local film community to stage the fake death that also served as a lesson to show kids contemplating a life of crime what was in store for them.

"The only reason I am standing on this stage instead of lying in a street is because I turned away from crime. I found my salvation in technology, but you can follow your own heart, whether it's in books or paintings or music or business. Follow the voice of passion, not the voice of violence."

The speech seemed to be going over well with the

crowd, even if Teddy thought the wording was a bit corny. Violence was as much a product of passion as music and painting, and history had shown that violence and art were more intertwined than society ever liked to admit. But Teddy kept those thoughts to himself as he strolled through the scene of *his* most recent violence.

♦ ♦ ♦

In the crush of bodies and screaming audience members, someone protected Li Feng. The woman, who had been part of the security crew for the film festival, escorted Li Feng out through a series of hidden access ways. They emerged on the opposite side of the chaos and caught their breaths before catching up.

"Thank you," Li Feng said.

"You should thank her, too," Dale said.

The woman named Millie Martindale from the CIA stepped into view. Dale Gai left the two of them alone.

"I was on my way over here to try and convince you one more time that I can protect you better than Arrow. Sounds like you're ready to believe that now."

"He had his man Bingo try to kill me."

"I have a car ready to take you to the airport right now," Millie said.

"My family has eyes at the airport. They have eyes everywhere. Arrow has eyes everywhere. The only way I was able to get in and out of the country before undetected was using Arrow's private plane."

"Don't worry about Arrow. He's not going to be a

problem anymore. We'll make a stop first. I know a guy who's pretty good with disguises."

"But my papers. My new identity. You can make me look like whoever you want, but my passport will betray me. My identity will betray me."

"This is what we do at the CIA," Millie said. "It's called extraction, and we're one of the best agencies in the world at it."

"I'm not a good person. I'm a terrible person."

"In exchange for getting you out of Macau and giving you a new life, my government is going to give you plenty of opportunities to do the right thing."

"I'm going to have to testify for real this time?" Li Feng asked.

"Maybe not in front of a big room of politicians, but yes, you're going to have to tell some people what really happened, all of it, and who was really responsible."

"That sounds like a terrible idea."

"Well, I can't say I didn't try," Millie said. "I thought I saw something in you that was worth redeeming. I'll just leave you here. I have some cash I can give you, but I'm not sure how far that will go with everyone in the country looking for you."

Millie stretched her face in a mock terrified look. Li Feng rolled her eyes and followed her latest ally into a waiting car.

"You made your point. Well done. Let's go see your magical disguise friend."

68

WHEN ARROW HADN'T HEARD ANYTHING FROM HIS DRIVER or from Li Feng after he saw the chaos unfolding, he got on the phone with his own contacts and found out what happened. It sounded like everyone was dead, and it felt like time to leave Macau and return home to the U.S. He could eat real American food and bask in his new monopoly on cell phone equipment in rural areas that would provide him massive business income as well as the opportunity to do the kind of lucrative spying on American citizens he'd been ready to blame on China.

He called the business airport and arranged for a flight back to Los Angeles. If nothing else, he could lay low on the beach until this all blew over, then see what his next move should be.

The flight was smooth, and Arrow slept soundly until

they landed the first time. He was sleeping so well he would not even have awakened had he not gotten an urgent alert on his phone from his accountant. Arrow couldn't get a cell signal but could check his voicemails. His accountant, not normally a man prone to dramatic outbursts, had left an exclamatory three-word voicemail.

"Check. Your. Accounts!"

Arrow logged on to his laptop, which was connected to the plane's Wi-Fi. He pulled up his accounts. All of them were empty. Still unable to get cell service, Arrow clicked the video conferencing app on his laptop and within a few seconds was staring at the haggard face of his accountant.

"How did this happen?"

"Some of it seems frozen by the government, but most of it seems like it was looted by someone who gained access to your personal accounts and all the money stored in the online casino's accounts. Everything is gone."

"Trace it!" Arrow screamed.

"We're working on it, but it's going to take time. This is very sophisticated and, as I mentioned, some of it has been frozen by the government so I would expect a visit from them soon."

Arrow quickly disconnected the video chat and went to grab his pilot so they could get back in the air before they were found. As he peeked his head out of the cabin door onto the landing strip, he knew he was done. A mixed group of uniformed and plainclothes officers was approaching. One of them, the FBI agent he'd seen talking to the CIA girl at the warehouse, was out in front of the group and coming toward Arrow.

"I'm Quentin Phillips with the FBI and this is a warrant to search your plane and any electronic devices on board and on your person."

"Where are we? This isn't legal. Where's my pilot?"

"This is less about where we are and more about where you're going," Quentin said.

"And where is that?"

"Back to the U.S. to be tried."

Arrow took a step back into the plane and wondered how long it would take for him to get the door shut and locked and if it would be quick enough to keep the cops off of the plane. He had no idea how to fly the plane and there were no weapons onboard that he knew of that could be used for a shootout so finally he gave up and put his hands in the air.

69

TEDDY WAS STANDING OUTSIDE OF THE SAFE HOUSE WHEN he saw the ugliest vintage limousine coming down the drive and he knew Millie and Li Feng had arrived. Millie quickly ushered Li Feng into the safe house and the car drove away. Teddy had all of his luggage open and ready to go with makeup, hair, and costume.

Teddy gave directions to Millie on how to get started with the physical props while he handled the most complicated part. He opened an app on his phone that he'd designed and had Li Feng put each of her fingerprints onto the scanner one at a time, and then he used a special camera filter to take pictures of her face front on and at various angles around the side and even the top of her head. The last two pictures were close-ups of her eyes.

As he waited for the photos to upload to his server, he watched Millie in her element getting Li Feng into her new identity. Teddy was never one for the mentor-protégé relationship, but he'd also never met anyone as talented and stubborn as Millie Martindale. Even more than the spy stuff, she seemed to have a genuine gift for the makeup and costume aspect of the job. With her more engaging personality she could move freely between a job in the CIA and the movie industry if that was something that interested her.

"I know you like the field work and adventure of your current job," Teddy said, when Millie came over to ask him a question about a piece of Li Feng's makeup she was struggling with, "but do you have any interest in working in the movies?"

"You mean like as a consultant or something? I think the Agency has a policy against that until you retire, and I'm not ready to retire yet."

"Part of it would be as a consultant, sure," Teddy said, "but I'm thinking something more off the books."

Millie froze what she was doing and turned back slowly to look at Teddy.

"You have my interest," she said.

"I haven't put too much thought into this yet, but we'd have to start with some kind of accident that would get you kicked out of the Agency officially, then you'd go off the books to work on stuff with me both on set and in the field."

"Could I get a new name, too? I want to be a stuntwoman, too, and maybe one of those people who blow things up on movie sets. How many identities do you have exactly?"

"Maybe this was a mistake," Teddy said. "Let's just finish up here and get our friend out of here safely."

"You can't just get me all excited for something and then take it away. Isn't that what got Li Feng all pissed at Sonny Ma? Right? Girl? Help me out here."

Li Feng avoided eye contact and Millie seemed to get the hint and went back to work.

"I'll take over here. My phone is plugged into the computer over there and all it needs is an official CIA login to get her new identity into the system."

"You're sure this will work?" Li Feng asked.

"The new set of papers waiting for you in the U.S. will match your regular appearance. This current look is designed to keep you from being identified by facial recognition software in the Macau airport and triggering you being held," Teddy said.

"One last thing," Millie said, handing Li Feng a notebook. "I need your written statement about Arrow bribing you to lie to Congress and any other of his crimes you may have been witness to."

Li Feng took the notepad and began writing. Millie typed in the information she needed to access the secure system for the CIA and then she and Teddy swapped places again so he could finish what he needed to do. When he was done, he did a once-over of Millie's costume work, which was exceptional, and said it was time to go.

"Have you done this sort of thing before?" Teddy asked Millie on the way out to a car he'd called for them.

"You mean dress up? It's all I did growing up."

"This is more than just dress up. This is . . . something else."

"I'm detail oriented. That's all it really is, right? You can't completely create a new person out of thin air, so you find the most common points on a person's face and body that form the rest of the identity and you disguise those."

"I can't wait to talk more with you about this," Teddy said. "And I have never said that to anyone ever that I can recall."

Li Feng handed the notepad back to Millie, who read the statement with her jaw on the floor.

"He did all of this?" Millie asked.

"That's how we met. He sent his people to tell me that QuiTel employees with high gambling debts at his casino were a security risk. So I put the company investigators on it and this is what I found. I kept all the documentation as a backup, in case he betrayed me."

"And you can prove all of this?"

She nodded and wrote something at the end of the statement.

"That's a secure website where I uploaded all of the documents. User name and password is there as well."

The car dropped Li Feng off at the airport and then took Millie and Teddy to the Macau Business Aviation Center.

"I hope you don't mind if I hitch a ride on your chartered flight," Teddy said.

"Why didn't we wait to find out if our plan worked?"

"I wouldn't have sent her in if I wasn't confident it would work."

70

DALE GAI WAS SURPRISED THAT ARROW HADN'T NOTICED his regular pilot had been replaced by a government agent, though on reflection it shouldn't have shocked her. A man like Arrow Donaldson barely noticed the underlings who propped up his entire life. She shook the pilot's hand and thanked him with a thick envelope of cash and headed to the car she'd arranged to take her to the Bank of the Philippines.

The interior of the bland concrete building was awash in the bright red and blue color scheme of the bank's logo, and Dale found herself a bit disoriented. She managed to find her way to the concierge banking area, which was plush and more subdued. Within minutes, a tall woman with quick speed and graceful posture joined her and escorted Dale to a cavernous office that seemed more like a rainforest-themed gift shop than a bank. They exchanged small talk while the woman typed, and finally, she wrote down a number in loopy, elegant script on creamy stationery and handed it to Dale. The amount was the balance in her accounts, just under a billion dollars. Dale wrote her own numbers down in a less elegant scrawl and handed the paper back. The numbers were a series of offshore accounts to which most of the money would be disbursed. The last was the amount Dale was requesting to withdraw in cash.

"Would you like some water or coffee while we get that prepared for you?"

Dale declined. Thirty minutes later the woman returned with a leather briefcase, which she handed over to Dale.

Briefcase in hand, Dale hailed a taxi and headed out to Manila Bay and a casino that looked like a giant glowing egg, where a suite was waiting for her. The next morning she had a meeting scheduled with the twenty-second richest person in the Philippines, who owned most of the McDonald's restaurants in the country, along with a small resort collection he was looking to expand that included properties in Singapore, the Philippines, and the Catskills in New York. She wasn't exactly sure what kind of role she was ready to play in his operation, but she was keeping all of her options open. Tonight, though, she would relax. First, she called a man in Macau to catch up.

◆ ◆ ◆

When Teddy finally made it back to L.A. without further trouble, he slept for the better part of three straight days. Millie Martindale had left a message inquiring about a threat assessment into her job and what sort of catastrophic injuries were common in her line of work that would result in her being pushed out. She also mentioned that she'd passed the information Li Feng gave her on to associates in other countries where Arrow would be facing additional charges.

"If he ever gets out of jail in the U.S., he's going to be passed around the world like a rotten oyster."

Teddy was having pancakes in Los Angeles when Dale Gai called. He wasn't even sure he wanted to answer. She'd left without saying goodbye, leaving him to clean up the various messes they'd been dealing with in Macau. He figured he'd misread some signals, and that in truth she wanted nothing other than a professional relationship. Then he remembered the electricity in the car ride and the touching of skin, and he answered the call.

"It turns out I came into some money and don't have anyone to help me spend it," she said.

"Is that money the reason you left without saying goodbye?"

"Oh my, you're not that type, are you? Neither of us ever believed this was going to be *Casablanca* with a big weepy ending."

"I've never been a big fan of *Casablanca*," Teddy said.

"Me neither. That's why we got along so well and why I think you should come visit me."

"And where would that be exactly?"

"Why should we start making it easy for the other to find out anything about us now?"

"Aside from looking for someone to help you spend that money, have you considered possible investment opportunities?"

"Do you have a pyramid scheme you'd like me to get in on?"

"Something even less stable than a pyramid scheme: the movies."

"You're really sticking to that movie producer bit?" Dale asked.

"It's not a bit, it's who I am," Teddy said. "It might be the truest version of myself."

"In that case, I have actually thought about it."

"What would make you do it?"

"The right partner," she said. "And the right story."

"I've got plenty of stories," Teddy said.

"When you're ready to be the right partner you can come and find me . . . Teddy Fay."

Before he could respond, the phone call was already disconnected. When he called the number back, a robotic voice told him the number did not exist.

When he was done with his pancakes, Teddy headed over to his office at Centurion Studios. He stopped along the way to pick up several bags of burgers and fries and American beer. He'd been away from home too long and was feeling patriotic. And hungry. When he arrived at the office, Peter, Ben, Stone, and Dino were chatting in the boardroom.

Teddy dropped the bags of food and the beer into the middle of the table and took a seat next to Stone.

The TV in the background was turned to CNN, which was showing the video of Teddy jumping from Macau Tower.

"You're a natural at that," Stone said. "You should be a stuntman instead of a producer."

They all laughed.

AUTHOR'S NOTE

I AM HAPPY TO HEAR FROM READERS, BUT YOU SHOULD know that if you write to me in care of my publisher, three to six months will pass before I receive your letter, and when it finally arrives it will be one among many, and I will not be able to reply.

However, if you have access to the Internet, you may visit my website at www.stuartwoods.com, where there is a button for sending me e-mail. So far, I have been able to reply to all my e-mail, and I will continue to try to do so.

Remember: e-mail, reply; snail mail, no reply.

When you e-mail, please do not send attachments, as I never open these. They can take twenty minutes to download, and they often contain viruses.

Please do not place me on your mailing lists for funny

stories, prayers, political causes, charitable fund-raising, petitions, or sentimental claptrap. I get enough of that from people I already know. Generally speaking, when I get e-mail addressed to a large number of people, I immediately delete it without reading it.

Please do not send me your ideas for a book, as I have a policy of writing only what I myself invent. If you send me story ideas, I will immediately delete them without reading them. If you have a good idea for a book, write it yourself, but I will not be able to advise you on how to get it published. Buy a copy of *Writer's Market* at any bookstore; that will tell you how.

Anyone with a request concerning events or appearances may e-mail it to me or send it to: Putnam Publicity Department, Penguin Random House LLC, 1745 Broadway, New York, NY 10019.

Those ambitious folk who wish to buy film, dramatic, or television rights to my books should contact Matthew Snyder, Creative Artists Agency, 2000 Avenue of the Stars, Los Angeles, CA 90067.

Those who wish to make offers for rights of a literary nature should contact Anne Sibbald, Janklow & Nesbit, 285 Madison Avenue, 21st Floor, New York, NY 10017. (Note: This is not an invitation for you to send her your manuscript or to solicit her to be your agent.)

If you want to know if I will be signing books in your city, please visit my website, www.stuartwoods.com, where the tour schedule will be published a month or so in advance. If you wish me to do a book signing in your locality, ask your favorite bookseller to contact his Penguin representative or the Penguin publicity department with the request.

If you find typographical or editorial errors in my book and feel an irresistible urge to tell someone, please write to Sara Minnich at Penguin's address above. Do not e-mail your discoveries to me, as I will already have learned about them from others.

A list of my published works appears in the front of this book and on my website. All the novels are still in print in paperback and can be found at or ordered from any bookstore. If you wish to obtain hardcover copies of earlier novels or of the two nonfiction books, a good used-book store or one of the online bookstores can help you find them. Otherwise, you will have to go to a great many garage sales.

TURN THE PAGE FOR AN EXCERPT

After a rocky jaunt in Maine, Stone Barrington is settling back in New York City when an old client reaches out for help with a delicate matter. A feud they thought was put to rest long ago has reemerged with a vengeance, and reputations—and money—are now on the line. In both the underbelly and upper echelons of New York, everyone has something to hide—and if Stone has learned anything, it's that history has a way of repeating itself . . .

1

STONE BARRINGTON HIPPED HIS WAY OUT OF A CAB (THE Bentley was being serviced) and found a discreet doorway with a polished brass number. He rang a bell and was answered by a silken female voice. "How may I help you?" She made it sound more like a bordello than what he was looking for.

"Stone Barrington to see John Coulter."

"Please come in." A buzzer gently sounded.

Stone entered the doorway, which led him to another doorway, that led to a comfortably furnished sitting room—Chesterfield sofa, etcetera—which made the place seem more like an exclusive gentleman's club. A young woman in a Chanel suit sat behind a large, mahogany desk. "Good morning," she said, identifying herself by her voice as the person Stone had heard on the intercom. "Mr. Barrington?"

"Yes."

"Will you follow me?"

That turned out to be an unexpected pleasure, as the suit was snug and its contents shapely. She led him to a door bearing a placard with a brass plate: LARK was imprinted upon it. She knocked gently, but firmly. There was a muffled response, then she opened the door and stood back for Stone to enter first.

The room was akin to a junior suite in an upscale boutique hotel. Once the door had closed behind him, he found that even the hospital bed was made of mahogany, as was the rack beside it, from which a pair of IV bags were draped. The lighting was pleasant, without the usual glare, a cheerful conflagration burned in a gas fireplace and a silk dressing gown hung from a peg on the wall near the foot of the bed.

"Stone?" a man's voice asked. "Is that you? It hurts to open my eyes." The man was unidentifiable, because of a large bandage across the bridge of his nose.

"It is I, Jack. I hope you feel a good deal better than you look."

"They just gave me some morphine. It will kick in shortly, then I'll feel human again." Jack Coulter's voice was the well-modulated, upper-accented baritone Stone had expected.

"Ahhhh," Jack breathed.

"The morphine kicked in?"

"I'm probably going to become addicted before they let me out of here. Would you like a drink?"

"What, grain alcohol?"

"There's a bar in the cupboard over there." Jack waved a hand.

Stone opened the door and found a full wet bar—sink, ice machine, a row of Baccarat whiskey glasses and a dozen choices of libation. He found a bottle of Knob Creek bourbon, filled a glass with ice, then filled that with bourbon. "I'm not offering you one, because I don't think you should mix booze and morphine," he said.

"I don't need it," Jack said contentedly. "Have a seat."

Stone pulled up a well-padded, burnished leather armchair and sank into it. Jack seemed to doze for a moment. Stone took the opportunity to reminisce about his first encounter with the man who had walked into his office, in his Turtle Bay townhouse, a few years back. He was maybe six-four, 250, wearing a dated suit that he could barely button. He had had a haircut that had been inflicted entirely with electric shears, and had been carrying a large suitcase and a smaller, non-matching duffel. He was frightening, until he spoke, in a voice much like the one he used now. He was also a good storyteller.

His name was John Fratelli, he said, and he had been a guest at an upstate hostelry called Sing Sing, until early that morning. He had spent the past twenty-three years there and had served all his time, without application for parole.

That explained the haircut, Stone thought, and the

twenty-three years explained the suit. Stone inquired as to why he had not accepted parole. Fratelli explained that he had had an obligation to protect a fellow resident, who was smaller and weaker than he, and who had been in increasingly delicate health for the past three years. A few days earlier, he had died in his bed. His name was Eduardo Buono.

Fratelli's name meant nothing to Stone, but Buono's rang a loud bell. He had been the mastermind behind the heist of fifteen million dollars from a currency-handling operation at John F. Kennedy Airport, after which he had distributed half the take among a half dozen abettors, then vanished into the mists with the other seven and a half million, after instructing them not to spend a penny of the money for a year. They had, of course, paid off their bookies, were fitted with new wardrobes, and drove shiny new Cadillacs off dealers' lots—all this in the first two weeks after their score. When arrested and confronted with their misdeeds and the sentences they would probably draw, they had ratted out, as the expression goes, their benefactor, Eduardo Buono, who thereafter never said a word to anybody until he met John Fratelli, on the bus from Rikers Island to Ossining.

The two men had bonded on the drive up, to the point where Buono had confessed to his new friend that he was terrified of being raped in prison and sought his help in avoiding that fate. Fratelli's mien was imposing enough that few challenged him, and Buono had served his time virginally. Late in his life he gave Fratelli a reward for his fealty, the name and address of a New York

City bank and the number of a large safe-deposit box and its key, which had resided for better than two decades in the orifice he had been so anxious to protect.

Fratelli said he had just come from the bank.

Stone had looked at the man's tatty luggage with new respect and discovered what appeared to be two bullet holes. Fratelli said that someone had gotten there ahead of him and had been waiting when he left the bank.

For the next hour or so, the two men had conducted a wide-ranging discussion, under the protection of attorney-client privilege, on the means of disappearing from New York City, arriving in a place where Fratelli could be more anonymous, change his identity and make more secure banking arrangements. Stone had also directed him to Brooks Brothers, where he could find apparel more suitable to the current quarter of the century.

Stone had heard from Fratelli sporadically, piecing together his story from their chats over the years. Fratelli had lost weight, grown hair, opened an offshore account, and met a very nice woman and her family, who were people of means. A few months later Stone had attended their wedding, and they had settled down in Hillary Coulter's Fifth Avenue apartment. The next time Stone had seen them was at a large dinner party in that apartment, during which men with shotguns had entered and relieved all present of their jewelry. Jack Coulter had thought people from his past had done it, but that turned out not to be true.

"Stone," Jack said, waking from his reverie. "I expect you want to know how I got here."

"If you'd like to tell me, Jack."

"Michael O'Brien," he explained.

O'Brien had been among the detectives investigating the robbery, and he thought he had recognized Coulter as Fratelli. Stone had disabused him of that notion, and they had heard no more about it, until now.

"Tell me how it happened," Stone said.

2

JACK COULTER SAID HE HAD BEEN WALKING UP LEXINGTON Avenue, alone. "I had just had a haircut and manicure at my regular barbershop, Nino's, in a hotel around the corner," he said. "I was shoved from behind. When I turned to look at the source of the aggravation, I caught a brief glimpse of O'Brien's face, then I was struck in the face by what I believe to have been a blackjack. The next thing I remember was my wife, Hillary, bending over me and saying that an ambulance was on the way."

"How did Hillary happen to be there?"

"She was walking down Lex in the opposite direction and saw a crowd of people hovering over someone, who turned out to be me. I passed out again and woke up in this hospital. Hillary knew the place, because she had a facelift here a couple of years ago. They specialize in facial work, and she wanted me to have the best possible nose man."

"I'm sure it will be fine, once you're healed," Stone said.

"The doctor says it will be better than fine. He worked from some old photos of me that Hillary had on her iPhone. He says people won't recognize me with my new nose."

"That sounds good. How long before it goes on display?"

"A couple of weeks or so," Jack said. "I'll have to wear a plastic cup over it for a while, so as not to frighten people. Right now, without the bandage, I've got two black eyes, and look like a raccoon."

"I look forward to meeting the new you."

"I thought, as long as I have to wear a disguise for a couple of weeks, I might as well find Detective Michael O'Brien and kill him."

"Whoa, there, Jack," Stone said. "That won't solve anything; you'd be in worse trouble than before. I take it O'Brien wants your seven million dollars."

"It's a lot more than that now. I invested wisely."

"I should consult you for stock tips," Stone said.

"I can introduce you to a friend from childhood who operates out of South Florida. If you've got a million to invest, he'll get you five percent a week."

"He must be one hell of a stockbroker," Stone said.

"He's a loan shark, who works for the biggest bookie in the state of Florida. The bookie feeds him a steady flow of borrowers."

"Well, that's interesting, but not for me. Do you think it's a secure means of investing?"

"Well, he doesn't know my new name or where I am. His organization sends couriers with cash to various offshore banks, then they wire my five percent to my offshore account."

"They have that account number?"

"There's one account number set up for deposits, and a different one for withdrawals."

"Suppose your, ah, lending friend or his boss should just decide to keep your million and not pay?"

"They know I can find them. Before I was incarcerated I had a mostly undeserved reputation for personal violence, mainly because of my appearance, which, you may remember, was more fearsome then."

"Fearsome it was," Stone said.

"I think it will be less so when I have healed."

"Then it might be a good idea to lie low until you do."

"We're going to spend a few weeks at Hillary's place in Northeast Harbor, Maine," Jack said. "We won't be going out."

"I think you know that I knew Michael O'Brien before his retirement from the NYPD." Stone said.

"I do."

"He was a very good detective, and was noted in the squad for his perseverance. Once on a case he was like a dog with a bone—he never, never let go."

"Then I may have to revert to plan A," Jack said. "Don't worry. I won't shoot him down in the street. I know people who know people who would take care of it."

"Jack, are you looking for a free ticket back to Sing Sing?"

"Don't worry about me, Stone. Come to dinner when we get back. I'll introduce you to my new nose." Then Jack dozed off again.

◆ ◆ ◆

Stone and his old NYPD partner, Dino Bacchetti, now the city's police commissioner, were dining at P. J. Clarke's, where the noise level covered their conversation. Since Dino was the only other person who knew about Jack Coulter's identity, with the possible exception of Michael O'Brien and anyone else he might have told, Stone could speak freely. He told Dino about the sudden alteration of Jack's appearance.

"It's ironic," Dino said, "that the only person who is hunting down John Fratelli is the one responsible for making him unrecognizable."

"Let's hope," Stone said. "We haven't seen the results of the surgery yet."

"Responding to your request, I got a report on O'Brien's behavior just before and after his, ah, retirement from the NYPD."

"Oh, good. I take it the retirement wasn't entirely voluntary."

"It was explained to him that he had two choices: he could go to trial on charges of abetting the robbery at

Jack Coulter's apartment, or he could turn in his papers and live out his life with a decent pension."

"You're satisfied that O'Brien is the guy who tipped the robbers to the gathering of all that expensive jewelry?"

"By a process of elimination, yes. I'm not sure we would win at trial, but we could indict him, and that would ruin him in the department."

"What information do you have on O'Brien's existence since he turned in his papers?"

"He's been doing rather well, except for the part about being a degenerate gambler."

"Where's he getting all the money he's losing?"

"His mother."

"I somehow thought he was from a fairly poor family."

"He was, until his father died and his mother remarried, and rather well. She was the cashier at a good restaurant downtown. Her boss fell in love with her and, after she was widowed, they were married."

"How much of a gap between husband one and husband two?"

"Not much. And husband two was very well off when he died a couple of years later. She sold the restaurant to some of their employees and gave them a mortgage, so she has a fine income—at least, what she can keep out of Mike's hands."

"Has anybody explored the convenient death of husband one?"

"It has been suggested that she may have helped him

along toward that goal, but there is insufficient evidence to charge her."

"I would imagine that her son could have been a great help to her in knocking him off, being a cop and all."

"We imagined that, too, but again, we couldn't prove it."

"Still that possibility might be something that could be dangled over O'Brien's head to keep him straight."

"Keeping him straight is important, I gather," Dino said.

"Suffice it to say that the Coulters are leaving town for a couple of weeks, until his new nose emerges. After that, he believes, he'll be harder to spot on Lexington Avenue."

"Good. Does that end the necessity of this conversation?"

"No. Jack has expressed an interest in removing O'Brien from the planet on a permanent basis."

"Then . . . Which one are we trying to protect?"

"Coulter, who, if he had his way, would endanger his personal freedom."

"You think Mike will forget about this while he's gone?"

"No. If you ever worked a case with O'Brien—"

"Several."

"Then you will recall his perseverance in pursuit of a suspect."

"Oh, yeah. Right."

"Also, if the reports you heard about his gambling habit are true, he is in perpetual need of money. And he may have worn out his welcome with his mother. I think he sees the downfall of Jack Coulter as the source of a windfall of funds."

"Well, there is the seven million Jack liberated from Buono's safe-deposit box, isn't there?"

"Jack says it's a lot more, now. A loan shark of his early acquaintance is sending him 50 Gs a week in interest on a million bucks Jack invested with him. And, as you know, Jack has been married to a very wealthy woman for some years now."

"All that makes him low-hanging fruit for O'Brien?"

"Obviously."

"And Jack is sure it was Michael?"

"Two things: First, a blackjack is a police weapon, albeit an illegal one in most circumstances. Second, Jack caught a glimpse of O'Brien immediately before he was struck."

"So," Dino said, "what is it you want—or rather, want me—to do?"

STUART WOODS

"Addictive . . . Pick it up at your peril. You can get hooked."

Lincoln Journal Star

For a complete list of titles and to sign up for our newsletter, please visit prh.com/StuartWoods